NO ONE TO HEAR
YOU SCREAM

NO ONE TO HEAR YOU SCREAM

•

K. J. Dahlen

AVALON BOOKS
NEW YORK

Published by Avalon Books,
an imprint of Thomas Bouregy & Co., Inc.
160 Madison Avenue, New York, NY 10016

Library of Congress Cataloging-in-Publication Data

Dahl, Kim.
    No one to hear you scream / Kim Dahl.
        p.   cm.
    ISBN 978-0-8034-7709-4
    1. Serial murderers—Fiction.   2. Murder—Investigation—
Fiction.   I. Title.
    PS3604.A339N6 2010
    813'.6—dc22

                                            2010022416

PRINTED IN THE UNITED STATES OF AMERICA
ON ACID-FREE PAPER
BY HADDON CRAFTSMEN, BLOOMSBURG, PENNSYLVANIA

*In loving memory of Nick and Janet Armoto
and Betsy and Raymond Dahl*

Acknowledgments

Thank you to my loving husband Dave, who encouraged me to write, and my best friends Carol and Tessi, who correct my mistakes and are always there for me when I need them.

Chapter One

To catch a killer you have to think like a killer, Sam thought as he stared at the trees surrounding the cemetery. It was quiet here, almost peaceful, and Sam knew that Chloe would have liked it if she could have seen it.

They were standing around the grave belonging to his wife, Chloe. His mother-in-law, Tessa, touched his arm. The small service they'd had for Chloe was over, and it was time to go home.

Sam didn't know if he could go back to the home he'd shared with Chloe and Wyatt. Chloe had turned the house into a home, and that home into a safe haven. Now that safe haven was gone. It wouldn't be the same without her, and she would never be there again.

Without looking at Tessa, Sam told her, "I want you to keep Wyatt for a while."

Tessa was taken aback. "What on earth for?"

Sam looked out over the graveyard. It was the time of year when all the lush greens they were so used to were being seared by the sun and turning brown. All the

1

brilliant colors were fading just a bit, sort of like the way he felt right now. His heart felt shriveled up and burnt, and all the color of his world was fading fast. He knew that his six-year-old son needed him, but Sam felt compelled to get the man who had killed Chloe. He turned to Tessa. "I want my son to be loved. He just lost his mom. I love him, but right now I have some things to do, and they may take a while. I want to know that Wyatt is taken care of. You can give him what he needs better than I can right now."

Tessa looked worried. "What are you going to do?"

Sam's face hardened and he growled, "I'm going after the monster who killed Chloe."

Alec Hunter, Sam's partner, joined them. "How are you going to do that? One minute he's here, and the next he's gone. We don't know where he is until his next kill. Besides, it's against the rules and you know it."

"I'll find him," Sam vowed. The rage he felt inside burned his soul. He turned to his partner. "Don't try and stop me. I have to do this, rules be damned."

Alec shook his head. "You are a law enforcement officer in New Orleans. For all we know, he could be in Mississippi or Texas by now. How are you going to track him?"

"I'll find him," Sam told them. "I'll track him down to hell if I have to."

"Daddy," Wyatt touched his arm. "I don't want you to go."

Sam looked down at his son. Wyatt's eyes, full of unshed tears, were so like his mother's that it almost broke Sam's heart.

He squatted to Wyatt's level, searching for the right words. He didn't know if Wyatt would understand, but he had to try. "Hey buddy, I know how you feel. I know this will be hard for you to understand. I hate that I have to leave you right now, but if I don't, the man who took your mom away from us is going to hurt someone else. I have to try to stop him." Sam paused to see if Wyatt understood. Tears rolled down his face. His son was hurting, and Sam was torn. He desperately wanted to stay, but he knew that if he did, the monster who had taken Chloe's life would disappear.

Sam pulled Wyatt into his arms and hugged him. "You know, don't you, that you and your mom mean the world to me?" Sam asked his young son.

When Wyatt nodded, Sam told him, "And you know that I'm a cop and that I make sure everybody obeys the law, don't you?"

When Wyatt nodded again, Sam leaned back and raised Wyatt's chin to look into his face. "When that man took your mom away from us, he broke the law. If I don't try to catch him, he's going to hurt other people, and he won't stop until somebody like me makes him. Do you understand?"

Wyatt thought for a moment, and then nodded.

Sam breathed a sigh of relief. What he was facing was going to be tough enough, with or without his son's cooperation. "Then you understand why I have to go?"

Wyatt looked down at Sam's chest for a moment, then looked up. "But what if this bad man hurts you the way he hurt Mom?"

Sam's arms tightened around his son. "He won't have the chance to hurt me. I'll be very careful, and I'll even make you a promise. I promise that when the bad guy is in jail, I'll come back to you."

Wyatt looked at him. He knew his dad never promised anything he couldn't deliver. "Ok, I'll stay with Grandma, but please hurry and come home again."

Sam smiled. "I'll be back as soon as I can."

Shortly after that, Sam went home to pack for his trip. He didn't give himself time to think about what he was doing, because if he did he never would have been able to go. He knew Wyatt needed him, but Sam needed to find Chloe's murderer. That was the only thing he could think about right now.

A few hours later, a jarring motion brought Sam out of a daze as his car hit the edge of the highway. He corrected his driving and pulled off the road. The near accident brought him back to his senses. His late start and the energy-draining last few days had left him too tired to get very far. He needed to get a room and some sleep. And he needed to check his e-mail anyway. He had found the killer's trail from the national police network and was on his way north to Baton Rouge to try and pick it up.

He got back on the road and found a motel in the first town he came to. Once in his room, he checked his e-mail. He had three messages.

One was from FBI agent Cole Davidson. Sam opened the message and scanned its contents. The FBI was after Chloe's killer as well. Several killings in and around Louisiana, Mississippi, and Arkansas had been linked to him, and Cole wanted to meet and compare notes.

Sam snorted. The FBI wasn't known to share anything, let alone information on a multistate killer. More than likely, Cole wanted to know what he knew, and when Sam told him, Cole would tell Sam to back off his investigation. Sam had already been through that with another case, and when he'd backed off, the suspect had gotten away and murdered two more women before he was caught. He'd been caught by good old-fashioned police work, not by the FBI. Sam wasn't going to let that happen again, not with this case. The FBI just didn't want him to get to the killer first.

The next message was from Alec. Sam frowned as he read the e-mail from his partner. Alec reported that just after Sam left, an FBI agent named Cole Davidson had paid him a visit. According to Alec, Cole wasn't happy about Sam looking for his killer. Alec warned him to watch his back; there was something about Cole that he didn't trust. Alec was a good judge of character, and if he had concerns, maybe Sam should check it out.

His third message was from Wyatt. Sam felt a moment of regret when he thought about his son. He'd hated leaving Wyatt, but he couldn't do what he had to and stay with the boy. He smiled at the message his son had written. He quickly wrote back and signed off.

After turning out the light, Sam lay down and let his mind clear.

At that precise moment, about twenty miles down the road, a shadowy figure moved from the edge of the Mississippi River, watching the shimmering lights of Baton Rouge. He was hungry tonight and in the mood for blood. His hand rested on the knife at his hip. The ivory handle felt smooth against his hand and as he lifted the knife out of its sheath, the blade of the double-edged dagger gleamed in the moonlight. He looked back at his home away from home. The sleek houseboat had everything a man could want. The improvements he'd made had been necessary and well worth the trouble.

He turned his dark eyes on the lights of the city again and stepped into the shadows as he made his way toward it. He was hunting for just the right woman, and he knew he would have to get her back to the houseboat before the sun came up in a few hours. Once on the boat, he'd have all the time he needed to do what he wanted. That was the fun part. What he was doing now was the necessary part.

He blended in with the city's night population, and as he made his way around the streets he searched for his prey. Suddenly he stopped and sniffed the air. A scent caught his attention. Looking around, he zeroed in on her.

She was slender, with flowing hair that reached her waist. Her beautiful skin glowed as she danced in the street. He was drawn to her infectious smile and laughter. As she swirled to the beat of the music, her dress flared and he could see the tops of her thighs. His blood raced as he stepped up to her.

Her eyes widened when he stepped close, but the music had gotten under her skin, and she smiled at him as they moved to the rhythm of the sounds that surrounded them. He was lost in the movement of their bodies and didn't realize at first that the music had stopped. When he did, he felt the world crashing down. She just smiled and swirled away from him, rejoining her own friends.

He moved off the dance area but stayed close to her, keeping her in sight until she showed signs of wrapping up the festivities. Her friends waved a weary good night, and she was left alone to walk home.

He followed from a safe distance until they were alone on the street. He swept down on her, and before she could scream his hands were around her throat. He put just enough pressure on her windpipe to close it off, but not enough to bruise the tender skin.

He let up when he felt her slump against him, and sticking to the shadows, he carried her limp form back to his boat. Once aboard, he laid her on the sofa and maneuvered the boat out of the main channel and into a backwater area.

He picked her up again and carried her to his special room. It was soundproof, and he had specially fitted it with his own toys.

A few hours later, the sun peeked over the eastern horizon. Sam came awake with a jerk. At first he couldn't remember where he was, and when he did he glanced at his watch and got out of bed. He checked his e-mail for additional messages while he got dressed. The only message was from Cole Davidson. The FBI agent insisted that Sam contact him as soon as possible. Sam was getting more than a little irritated by the agent's demands. He closed his laptop and turned on the television. The local news was just announcing the disappearance of a young woman, seen the night before dancing in the street with her friends.

Sam was transfixed by the sight of the young woman dancing and swaying to the music. She was the same height and build of his Chloe. Chloe had the same long, dark hair when she was alive. It had been hacked off by the killer, and it wasn't found with her mutilated body.

The woman was just the killer's type, and Sam knew in his gut that he'd struck again. Sam was only a few miles from Baton Rouge. He quickly gathered his things. If he had any hope of finding this woman, he needed to get started before the killer finished the job. He had just closed the door and was walking away when the phone rang.

Alec held the phone receiver tightly, counting the rings on the other end. Cole Davidson stood right behind him, along with Alec's police captain, John Todd. After several more rings Alec hung up. "I don't think he's there anymore." He ignored Cole and looked at his captain for instruction.

John looked irritated. "Then you find him. Find him

and get his sorry butt back here. He knows better than this. I won't have a cop running around out there looking for vigilante justice."

Alec looked over at Cole and then back at his captain. "Sam isn't a vigilante, and he isn't out there looking for revenge. He's out there looking for the man who murdered his wife."

"So are we," Cole said quietly. "This situation is much bigger than just one woman. Sam's wife is only one of a number of women this monster has killed. We want to stop him without having to worry about a loose cannon out there."

Alec frowned. "Sam isn't a loose cannon. He's the best officer I know."

"Then why isn't he answering your phone calls or e-mails?" Cole asked. "This is the FBI's case, and we won't share it with a police officer with a wish to ruin four years' worth of work. I don't care who that officer is."

Alec didn't answer. He had known yesterday that Sam was embarking on a mission he shouldn't be. There was a good reason why doctors didn't operate on their relatives and why cops weren't allowed to assist on cases too close to their families. Alec had a feeling that Sam's anger might prevent him from acting according to the laws of the land.

Sam pushed open the door to the police station in Baton Rouge and walked into the lobby. As he made his way to the front desk, he could see several officers busy working.

The burly cop behind the desk paused to look up at him. "Can I help you?"

"I'm looking for information on the missing woman," Sam told him.

The man behind the desk looked at Sam for a moment and then called to another officer. As the other officer came to the counter, he too asked, "Can I help you?"

Sam pulled out his badge. "My name is Sam Sebastian, and I'm from New Orleans looking into a murder case that may be connected to your missing person report from last night."

The second officer held out his hand. "My name is Rob Gillette. What makes you think the cases are related?"

Sam shifted his weight. "Both women have the same build and coloring. Both seemed to enjoy life, and both disappeared in the same manner. The only difference is that mine ended up dead. I figure you have about thirty-six hours before you find what's left of this woman's body. You'll find that she bled to death from an elaborate design carved on her back. What you won't find is the original crime scene or the killer."

Rob's eyebrows rose, causing his forehead to wrinkle. "I think you'd better talk to my captain." He motioned for Sam to follow him to the back of the office, where he saw several officers gathered around a board. Sam stepped forward and read the information they had written on it. He picked up a marker and began changing the facts.

"Just what do you think you're doing and who are

you?" someone bellowed. Sam turned to see Rob talking to the man who had bellowed. They stepped up and Rob made the introductions.

"Boss, this is Sam Sebastian, from New Orleans. He told me he has information on our latest missing person case."

Rob's boss, Captain Ian Nevell, just stared at Sam. He turned his eyes to the changes Sam had made on their board. "How do you know all this?"

"I've been doing my homework. This is his fourth kidnapping since Easter. In about thirty-six hours you'll find her body. Her long hair will be cut off and her body will be mutilated by an elaborate design carved in her back. Your coroner will find that she's been tortured and that the carving on her back was made while she was alive."

Ian and Rob looked at each other. "This is our second kidnapping. We had one several months ago that we haven't solved. We haven't found her body yet, but there was enough evidence to suggest that she was taken against her will and no one has heard from her since. Her case fits this killer's MO. This latest case is pretty much the same as the earlier one."

"I'm surprised that the FBI isn't in on this yet," Rob commented.

"Yeah, well, an agent named Cole Davidson has been trying to get in touch with me, but I haven't had a chance to call him yet," Sam admitted.

Ian folded his arms across his chest. "Why not?"

"Maybe I just don't like Big Brother butting into my business. I have my own way of doing things." Sam shrugged.

"Well, we do things differently up here. If Big Brother wants to talk, we listen." Ian told him. "You need to find out what he wants."

"He doesn't have to. Big Brother is already here," came a voice from behind Sam.

Sam turned and came face to face with who he guessed was FBI agent Cole Davidson. Behind him stood Sam's partner, Alec Hunter. Alec gave him a short nod, and all attention turned to Cole.

"You're a hard man to get ahold of, Mr. Sebastian," Cole noted after introductions were made. He walked over to the board and spent a few minutes looking over the information. Picking up the pen, Cole began to write.

Alec took a moment to talk to his partner. "Sam, we tried to call your motel room this morning, but you didn't answer the phone."

"I left my room when I saw the news report. How did you know where I was staying?" Sam asked.

Alec grinned slightly. "Wyatt passed on the message you sent him last night."

Sam shook his head. "I know I should be home with him, but I can't just sit on my hands and do nothing." Sam turned away from his partner and began to read what Cole was writing on the board. "I couldn't let this case turn into another Sara Morgan screwup."

Alec nodded. He remembered the Sara Morgan case all too well. They were hours away from getting her killer off the streets when the FBI showed up and took over. They not only let the killer escape, but gave him enough time to strike again and again. It was Sam and another cop who finally busted the killer, but instead of thanking them, the FBI took credit for the collar. Now the FBI was horning in again, and this time Alec knew Sam wouldn't back off. Alec didn't blame him; catching this killer was too important. But Alec also knew that Sam had no real business investigating this case. It was too personal.

"What makes you think he uses the river as a means of transportation?" Sam asked Cole after a moment.

Cole paused in his writing and then resumed. He recapped the pen and threw it on the desk. "I've been looking for this killer for four years."

"He's been killing for that long?" Rob asked.

Cole nodded. "At first, he killed about every six months or so—it's just been lately that his killing has escalated. His last three murders have been about a month apart."

"His last murder was about ten days ago." Sam spoke very quietly. Alec was worried at his tone. He knew that when Sam spoke softly, trouble was brewing.

Cole looked over at Sam. "That's true, but I think your wife was just in the wrong place at the wrong time."

Ian jerked his head to look at Sam. "Your wife was one of his victims?"

Sam nodded.

"Then what are you doing working this case?" Ian asked.

Cole shook his head. "We really don't want you out there looking for this killer. We've got more man-hours in on this case than you could ever hope to have, and we'll get him eventually."

"I'm not about to let her killer go free so you can catch him *eventually*," Sam said. "And I don't care how many hours you have on this killer. You haven't found him yet. Maybe I will."

"You do realize that your relationship to one of the victims could affect your judgment, don't you?" Ian suggested.

Sam stiffened. "My judgment is just fine, thank you very much. I want this creep off the streets, hopefully buried six feet under them."

Nobody noticed the flash of pain in Cole's eyes at that statement. He couldn't let his secret be known, not just yet. He had too much to do first. He tried to speak, but the words wouldn't come. He cleared his throat and tried again. "That's what we don't want. We don't need you on a rampage, looking for trouble."

"You don't have to worry about me," Sam told him. "This is the closest anyone has gotten to the killer, and I don't intend to back off now."

"You may not have a choice," Ian warned Sam. "Not if you want to keep that badge."

Sam glared at Ian and said, "With or without my badge I would still be looking for this murderer."

"Do you want justice or vengeance?" Cole asked. Sam turned his glare on him. The silence in the room thickened with tension.

"Vengeance is not a part of this equation. I am going after a serial killer. That my wife was one of his victims is irrelevant. We know that he's responsible for at least seven other murders, and God only knows how many we haven't found yet. As an officer of the law, I can't let that go, and I won't. I let your people take over one of my cases already, and they screwed up. That won't happen again, not with this case."

Cole glanced away. The animosity between the two men was apparent, and Cole knew he had to back off if he wanted to salvage what was left of his case. Besides, if they knew what he knew about this killer, he would be in the same position as Sam, and that wouldn't do. If the killer had murdered his wife, he wasn't sure he could leave the case alone either. Cole knew that Sam wouldn't back off, but neither would he. This case was important to him as well, but for a different reason.

He glanced over at Rob and asked, "What do we know about his latest victim?"

"Her name is Sable Willows."

Cole looked over at Ian and nodded. "We'll need access to a boat to check all the backwaters in this area. If he's still around here, we should be able to find him."

As the police were getting themselves organized, a dark-haired man was entering a café just a few blocks from the police station. He smiled at the waitress and ordered his usual breakfast, a cup of green tea and a bagel with cream cheese. As he sat there and sipped his tea, the other patrons would have been surprised at the thoughts running through his head. He was working out the design he would carve on the back of his current kidnapping victim. His dark eyes, so much like those of Cole Davidson, were lost in thought as the elements of the design swirled through his head.

Sable came to in a fog of unreality and confusion. Her throat hurt, and her right arm felt very heavy. She tried to pull it toward her but met with some resistance. Looking up, she saw that her right wrist was shackled. She frowned and tried to sit up. At first her head swam and she felt sick to her stomach, but after a few minutes her head cleared and she looked around.

The room was small, and she felt it dip and sway. Pulling on her wrist only tightened the rope. With her free hand, she tried to work the rope loose. She was able to loosen it enough to slip it off her wrist. She rubbed her bruised and raw wrist gently, and staggering, she went over to the window. She found herself looking out at the backwater bayou. It was dark out, and she didn't see anything familiar and couldn't get a fix on where she was.

She made her way over to the door and tried to open it. It was locked. Panic set in, and she kept pulling on the handle. She didn't want to be here when whoever had brought her here came back. The door wouldn't budge, so she went back to the window. It wasn't very big, but

Sable thought she could squeeze through it if she could get it open.

She looked for a lock on the window but couldn't find one. She picked up a small lamp from the bedside table and tried to smash the glass, but the tempered glass wouldn't break, and there wasn't anything in the room hard enough to break it.

Suddenly she stopped struggling with the window and peered outside. An outboard motorboat was coming her way.

The passenger was alone. Somehow she knew it was her kidnapper. She watched as he removed his black cowboy hat and wiped the sweat from his forehead. Fear swelling within her, Sable caught her breath. She knew he was going to kill her. Why else would he have brought her so far into the backwaters?

Then her eyes hardened. She wasn't going to let the monster win. He might kill her, but she would go down fighting. She went over to the door and heard him come aboard the boat. Her eyes darted around the room looking for something, anything, to strike the first blow. She caught sight of a heavy glass vase of flowers. Dumping the flowers on the floor, she raised the vase and waited. Her eyes were glued to the slowly turning doorknob. She took a deep breath.

Chapter Two

He came into the room and stopped short. The bed he had tied her to was empty. Surprise caused him to hesitate, and that's when Sable brought the heavy vase down on his skull. The pain exploded in his head, and for a brief moment he couldn't see, it hurt so bad. He staggered and would have fallen to the floor, but he grabbed hold of the bed instead. He reached for the knife he had hidden on his right side and swung it toward her.

Sable dodged the arc of the knife and raised the vase to hit him a second time. The knife slashed at her once more, this time piercing her skin. She screamed but managed to bring the vase down on him again. It broke and he collapsed. He was still for a moment, and Sable wondered if she'd killed him, but she wasn't about to wait around and find out. She stumbled through the door and off the boat. She got into the outboard motorboat and pulled on the cord to start the motor. She turned the little boat away from the houseboat and got out of there.

Sable didn't know if she was headed toward land or

away from it. Her side was bleeding, but she was determined to survive. All she knew for certain was that she had to get away from him.

A while later, she made another turn and found herself in the main part of the river. She could see a large area of lights nearby, and she headed the little boat toward the lights. Bumping against the shoreline a few minutes later, she stumbled onto shore and made her way toward the lights. She had no idea where she was going—only that there were probably people ahead of her. She knew that if her kidnapper survived the head injury, he was just behind her and she had to put as much distance between them as she could.

About fifteen minutes later, she stumbled into the middle of the street. She could see and hear the people near her, but she was unsure of where she actually was. When the people nearby saw the blood on her clothes, they tried to get away from her. She saw their faces and felt their fear. Breathing heavily by this time, she was about to pass out from the loss of blood when she felt someone's arm take the weight of her own body. Opening her eyes, she saw a face she didn't recognize. His blue eyes had concern and compassion in them, not the malice of her kidnapper.

"Please, I need to go to the police," she begged.

He frowned. "Are you sure you don't want to go to the hospital first?" the stranger asked her.

Sable shook her head. "Please, the police. The man who stabbed me is out there on the river, and I don't want him to get away."

The man nodded and looked around the neighborhood. He saw a station sign just ahead on the street. "There's a station not too far from here. Can you walk there?"

"I think so. Please don't leave me alone."

The stranger smiled. "I won't."

As he helped her down the street and into the police station, Sable knew time was of the essence. Even now her kidnapper could be watching her and waiting for her to be left alone. It was only when she was in the station house in a room full of people that she felt safe enough to let the stranger go. She lay her head back against the wall and let herself rest for a moment. The buzzing of conversation lulled her into a light sleep.

When she awoke a few hours later she noticed the beeping sound of a monitor and the smell of hospital antiseptic. How had she gotten here? She tried to sit up but she was in too much pain. Running her hand along her side, she felt a bandage. Had she fallen or fainted at the police station?

Sable looked around the room. She was alone, and that fact didn't bring much comfort. She tried to look at the clock, but it was just out of her line of sight. She didn't know why, but she felt she had to get out of the hospital. She was flinging back the sheets and swinging her legs over the side of the bed when the door opened. She jerked her head toward the door and was about to scream when two men walked into her room.

"Are you going somewhere?" the first man asked her.

Sable wet her dry lips with her tongue. Her fight-or-flight response kicked in, and she felt the adrenaline giving her body a sudden boost of energy. "Who are you guys, and what do you want?"

"We're the police," the second man told her gently. "You came to see us but passed out before we could meet."

"Can I see some ID, please?" Sable asked. She couldn't take her eyes off them, and she prayed she wasn't making a mistake by accepting their reason for being here.

Both men reached into their pockets for their badges. Flipping open their wallets, Sable could see they did have proper identifying badges. She could also see the badges were different from each other. "Why aren't they the same?"

The one named Rob smiled. "My friend here is from south Louisiana, but we are both working on your case."

Sable frowned. "I have a case?"

"What do you remember of the last day or so?" Sam, the other man, asked.

Sable lay back on the bed and pulled the sheets up. "I remember being out dancing with some friends. We had gone out to check out the jazz bands playing down by the river. Some guy in a black cowboy hat started dancing with me. At first it was a little freaky. I mean, he wore the hat down so low that the brim hid most of his face, but the music was loud and we'd been drinking a little, so I didn't really care. I finished the dance and went back to my friends. I didn't notice him again until I was walking home."

"Then what happened?" Sam asked.

Sable felt tears welling in her eyes. "I don't know. One minute I was walking down the street, and the next minute he jumped out of nowhere and his hands were around my throat. I tried to fight him off, but he was just too strong. I couldn't even scream for help, the attack happened so fast. I tried to struggle—I even clawed at his hands, but I couldn't get away from him. I managed to cry out. I could still hear the party going on a block away, but I couldn't call out loud enough for anyone to hear me. All I could see were his eyes. They were so black. When I struggled and tried to cry out, the blackness in his eyes got darker. It was like they were pulsing, and the more I struggled and cried out, the blacker they got. I could feel the darkness surrounding me. I know that doesn't make any sense, but that's the way I felt. I must have passed out, because the next thing I knew I was on a boat out in the middle of no-man's-land."

Rob looked at Sam with interest. "What kind of boat was it?"

"A houseboat, I think. He had me tied to a bed. I managed to get free, but I couldn't get out of the room. The door was locked, and the window did not open at all. I tried to scream for help, but no one heard me." Sable closed her eyes at the memory of how helpless she'd felt on the boat.

"What happened next?" Rob asked gently.

"I saw someone coming in a little motorboat, and I hid behind the door. When he came in, I hit him with a vase. It was the only thing I could find in the room. He went down, but he wasn't out. I had to hit him again, and that's when he sliced open my side. Anyway, I managed to get out of the room, and I stole the little boat and made it back to town. That's all I can remember." Sable's finger plucked at the hem of the sheet as she told her story.

"Don't worry, Miss Willows, you'll be safe here," Sam assured her.

"What if he comes looking for me? Who was he, and why did he want me?" Sable cried out in pain and confusion. "I don't even know this man."

"Unfortunately, we don't have any answers yet. When we catch up with your mystery man, we'll ask him," Rob told her. "We'll talk again later. The doctor says you've lost a lot of blood, so we'll leave you to rest."

Sable felt tired and soon drifted off to sleep. When she woke, the room was dark, but she knew she wasn't alone. She could hear him breathing. She could smell his cologne. Her heart was pounding in her chest, and the sound echoed in her head. Fear made breathing difficult and she wanted to run but she knew she couldn't. Her limbs were suddenly very weak. She was at his mercy, and she could only pray that someone would come into her room and tell her that it had only been a nightmare. She shifted her gaze and saw his silhouette in the chair in the corner of the room. Her breathing stopped as she fixated on the outline of a cowboy hat. She closed her eyes, hoping it would go away.

He got up from the chair where he was waiting for her and stepped over to the bed. Leaning down, he placed his hands on either side of her head. When her eyes sprang open, he could see the fear in them, and his black eyes took on an ungodly glow. "I found you. You should know that I will always find you. The police can't protect you from me. If they get in my way, I will kill them to get to you. We have some unfinished business to take care of, and I won't be stopped." He gently cupped her chin and tilted her face to his.

"Rest for now, but know that I'll be back for you. Any time, any place you go, I will find you, and the next time we meet, we'll finish what we started."

Chapter Three

Sable wanted to scream but fear was closing her throat. Her heart was beating so fast, she thought she would pass out. She closed her eyes and tried to breathe, but all she could hear was her own labored gasps. A few minutes went by, and when she opened her eyes, he was gone. The room was empty except for her. She found the light switch, and when the lights came on, she looked around. She was alone.

She knew she had to get away from the hospital. She had to go somewhere he couldn't find her. She sat up too fast and the room spun. Holding the sides of her head, the spinning finally stopped and she was able to push the sheets down. She yanked the IV out of her arm and got to her feet. Her arm was bleeding, but she couldn't worry about that right now. She had to get dressed and find a way to escape.

As the sun rose high enough to flood the town with light, Sam and Cole walked down the street toward the station house. Sam was hungry for the first time in days, so they were planning to stop for breakfast at the small café near the station. As they pushed the door open, they heard the familiar sounds of an eating establishment, the clatter of dishes, the clink of silverware, and the buzzing of conversation. They sat down at a booth and waited for the server to greet them.

"So what's your take on what happened yesterday?" Sam asked Cole.

"I think the fact that Sable got away from the killer was pure luck on her part," Cole told him.

"What do you mean by that?" Sam frowned. He didn't trust Cole, but there was an uneasy alliance between them. For now Sam was holding back his judgment of his true motive. When Sam had shown up at the police station this morning, he'd caught the look of irritation in Cole's eyes. He knew the other man didn't want him working this case, but Sam wasn't going to let that bother him. Sam sensed there was something Cole was holding back about the case, and he wasn't going to let that happen. Sam wasn't going to let anything stop them from finding this killer.

"I mean that this killer doesn't usually give up his victims until he's done with them. He never has before," Cole pointed out. "I have to find the men's room. I'll be right back."

Sam watched him leave the table and was lost in thought when the server brought coffee a minute later. The fact that she only brought one cup didn't register for a second. It wasn't until she brought out another cup, a little teapot, and a bagel with cream cheese and set it up where Cole had been sitting that Sam even noticed what she was doing.

"Excuse me, we haven't ordered yet," Sam told her.

The server, Millie, just smiled. "That's what he has every morning. Don't worry—I'll be back for your order."

Sam was still frowning when Cole got back. He sat down and looked at the food in front of him. Looking at Sam, he asked, "What's going on here? I didn't order this."

"According to the server, this is what you have every morning." Sam stared at him. "Is there something you're not telling us?" Sam's inner alarm was buzzing loud and clear, and he was listening.

Before Cole could respond, Sam's cell phone rang. He didn't take his eyes off Cole as he answered the call. He listened for a moment, then ended the call. "We'll deal with this later. That was Rob at the hospital. Sable is missing. We're supposed to meet him there."

A few minutes later, Sam and Cole rushed down the hospital corridor. They stopped short of the room Sable should have been in and found Rob just inside the doorway.

The room was in shambles. The bed was pushed out of the way; the sheets lay on the floor. The bedside table was overturned, and the water pitcher and glass were on the floor. The closet doors were open, and there was blood and water everywhere—on the bed, on the floor, and on the furniture. "This doesn't look good," Cole whispered as he ran his fingers through his dark hair. Sam just glared at him.

Rob nodded. "This is what I found a few minutes ago when I opened the door. I called in our crime scene investigators. They should be able to tell us something in a few hours."

"Sable may not have a few hours," Sam pointed out. She was weak from blood loss, and if the killer had gotten to her she could be dead. "Have you talked to any of the night nurses yet?"

Rob shook his head. "I called you first." He was about to make another comment when all three of them heard a gasp from behind them. Turning, they saw a young woman peek into the room.

"My God, what happened here? Where is Sable?" she asked them. She looked pale and her hands were shaking. She glanced around the room.

"I don't mean to be rude, but who are you and what are you doing here?" Sam asked her.

"My name is Callie St. Marie. Sable and I are friends. I heard she was found yesterday, so I came to see her." Callie paused and looked around the room again. "What happened?"

Rob nodded toward the room. "We don't know yet."

They all turned at the sound of footsteps hurrying down the hall. It was a nurse, her face expressing concern as she joined the group. "I'm sorry, but I've been busy. I was on my way out the door when the director told me you wanted to speak to me."

Sam read her name badge. "Kelly, did you see anyone entering or leaving this room last night?"

Kelly looked uncomfortable and wouldn't meet Cole's eyes. Instead she focused on Sam and Rob. "I did see someone leaving the area, but I couldn't say if he was actually in the room or not."

Sam frowned. "And what did this person look like?"

Kelly took a deep breath. "He was about six feet tall, with dark hair, a slim build, and a black cowboy hat."

Everyone's eyes turned toward Cole. "Does he look like the man you saw last night?" Sam asked suspiciously, pointing at Cole. Alarms were again ringing inside his head. It wouldn't be the first time a murderer posed as a law enforcer. The nurse's discomfort only reinforced the gnawing doubt Sam harbored about Cole Davidson.

"Yes," Kelly said quietly. "He does look a lot like the man I saw last night—except for the hat, of course."

Cole was shocked. He hadn't been near the hospital last night. "I was in my motel room all night. I watched part of a ball game, ordered a pizza, and went to sleep around midnight. Whoever it was she saw, it wasn't me."

Sam looked over at Rob, and they both looked at Cole. Sam was feeling uneasy about the coincidences regarding Cole that were piling up. All he had right now were questions without any answers.

"I think we need to get ahold of the original footage the news ran when Sable was missing. There has to be something on the video that we're missing," Sam told Rob.

"I have the video. In fact, it was my file that they aired," Callie told them.

Sam jerked his head to where Callie was standing. He'd forgotten she was there. "What did you say?"

"When Sable turned up missing, the local news station ran an alert asking for any information about when she was last seen. I provided them a copy of the footage I'd shot the night before," Callie explained. "I'm trying to break into journalism and I never go anywhere without my camera. I was trying to get a piece on Baton Rouge's night life."

"Do you have the original?" Sam asked.

Callie nodded. "I gave the news station a copy. They didn't run the whole thing, only the part with Sable dancing."

Rob handed her a business card. "Bring the file to this address as soon as you can. Also, we'll need a phone number where we can reach you, as well as a list of Sable's friends and family in the area—anything you can think of that will help us find her."

Callie took the card and hurried off. The nurse turned to leave as well. She had given Rob her name and home phone number and promised to be available if they needed additional information from her.

"We're going back to the station to see what we can get from a background search. That way we'll be there when Callie brings in the video," Sam told Rob.

"I'll wait here for the forensic team. I'll head back to the station when they finish up," Rob told them.

Sam and Cole walked down the hall toward the front

doors. Cole was bothered by the nurse identifying him as having been in the hospital last night. Both men were quiet as they walked down the hall, but tension was building between them.

Neither man was paying attention to the other people in the hall, so when one called out to Cole, he didn't stop. The man reached out and touched Cole's arm. "Nick? Is that really you?"

Cole jumped. "Excuse me?"

The man smiled. "I thought it was you. I called out twice. You must have been really deep in thought."

Cole looked confused. "Do I know you?"

The welcome on the other man's face faded a bit. "I'm Jerry Springs. Come on, man, it's only been three weeks since you worked for me."

"Excuse me, sir, but who do you think this is?" Sam asked.

"Nick Granger—his name is Nick Granger. He did some computer troubleshooting for my investment firm about a month ago," Jerry told them.

"Are you positive?" Sam asked.

"He spent three weeks in my office teaching the staff how to use the new software. I think I would recognize the man." Jerry was getting irritated. "What is going on here?"

Sam looked from Jerry to Cole and back again. He introduced himself to Jerry and asked for a business card. "We are investigating the disappearance of a young woman and we may need to get in touch with you."

Jerry took out his wallet. "I don't know anything

about a missing woman, but here's a card that has my work and home phone numbers on it. I'm here to visit my wife. We just had a baby, so if you need me I'll probably be here or at home."

"Thank you," Sam said as he pocketed the card. He watched as Jerry Springs made his way to the elevator, and when he disappeared Sam turned to Cole.

"That was strange. I swear I didn't know him, and I have never done computer troubleshooting," Cole assured him.

Sam was quiet as they passed through the front doors of the hospital. He didn't like where his thoughts were taking him. He had to find some answers.

Sam and Cole didn't say a word to each other all the way back to the station house. When they got there, Sam went straight to Captain Nevell's office. The captain wasn't there, so he sat down at his computer and began a background check on Sable Willows, a man named Nick Granger, and Cole Davidson. He had to find out if the FBI agent was hiding anything.

Nick Granger's home address was in a little town near New Orleans called Myrtle Grove. He would have to call Alec and get him to run Nick Granger down.

When Ian Nevell entered his office, he wasn't surprised to find Sam there. He sat down on the corner of his desk. "Cole told me what happened this morning."

"All of it?" Sam asked, shooting him one of those looks. It was the kind of look one person gave another when they were after the truth.

"What do you mean by that?" Ian wanted to know.

He knew the two men didn't like each other, but didn't know why.

"What exactly did he tell you?" Sam repeated his question without giving Ian any information of his own.

Ian looked at Sam for a moment. "He told me that while you two were at the café this morning, the waitress gave him a breakfast he didn't order and that she told you it was his normal breakfast. And while you were at the hospital, the night nurse claimed he was there during the night, and that on the way out some guy he'd never seen before stopped the two of you and claimed that Cole was actually a man named Nick Granger. Is that all of it, or did he leave something out?"

Sam nodded. "That's about all of it. At this point there seem to be more questions than answers, and now with our only witness on the missing list, we're back to square one."

"Well, maybe the boat patrol will turn something up," Ian told him.

"What boat patrol?"

"Last night before he went home, Rob ordered the police boat out on the river to check for the houseboat Sable told you guys about. They took off first thing this morning. They should be calling in any time now," Ian said. The phone in his office rang, and Sam got up to leave but Ian motioned him to stay. Grabbing a pen from the desk, he began writing down information. When he finished, he hung up the phone.

"They found the boat. In almost the same spot Sable

told you about. The patrol didn't see anyone aboard, but they didn't get too close to it. They did catch the registration numbers on the side of the boat. It belongs to a man named Paul Moran," Ian told him.

"I'll run a trace on Paul Moran and see what I can come up with," Sam told him.

"You might want to give Cole the benefit of the doubt. I spoke to his boss this morning, and Clayton Conway assures me that Cole is one of his best agents. He also said that if you could work together, you both might solve this case, but that if I thought there were going to be problems between you guys, neither one of you would end up on the case. Clay told me that the FBI has jurisdiction because of the multistate ruling and that Cole doesn't have to let you tag along," Ian told Sam. He held up his hand at the look on Sam's face. "I told him that if you didn't work this case, Cole was going to have you working against him all the way to its conclusion anyway."

Sam nodded. "That's for damn sure."

Ian nodded. "Then you have to play nice with him. Find a way and make it happen, or you'll be pulled off and Cole will do it alone."

Sam glared at him for a moment. Then he sighed and said, "I think Cole is hiding something. Maybe he knows something and doesn't realize it, or maybe he just doesn't want us to know everything. I don't know. Sometimes he seems to be two different people."

"See what turns up on Moran. Rob should be back

soon, and when he gets here fill me in." Ian nodded and closed the door to his office.

Using a computer at an unoccupied desk in the squad room, Sam began another background check on Paul Moran. The report came back almost immediately. Paul Moran was a boat salesman out of New Orleans.

Sam grabbed the phone and called Alec. Alec would be able to bring Paul in for questioning. Sam finally felt as if they were making progress on this case, or at least he hoped they were.

"Hunter," Alec answered his phone.

"Alec, this is Sam. I need you to run down something."

"Did you guys turn something up?"

"Maybe—I don't know yet. Listen, I need you to find a boat salesman by the name of Paul Moran. The New Orleans woman actually escaped and led us to a houseboat where the killer had kept her. The boat belongs to Paul Moran. I need you to find Moran and talk to him. I'm going to run a DMV photo of him. Oh, and can you run down to Myrtle Grove and see a man named Nick Granger? Both names have come up in this case, and I need to know more about these men."

"Anything else?" Alec asked. "How's your witness doing?"

"She's gone missing, and we don't know if she left by herself or if she was persuaded by someone that looks a great deal like FBI agent Cole Davidson," Sam told him.

"What are you talking about?" Alec sounded shocked.

"I'll fill you in later. Just get on tracking down those two names for me and call me back. I have another report coming in." Sam hung up the phone as the background check on Sable Willows was coming across the fax machine.

A few minutes later, Rob Gillette came through the station house door looking grim. He nodded for Cole and Sam to join him in Ian's office. Opening the door, they found Ian on the phone. He motioned for them to come in, and after he hung up he sat back in his chair. "Well, what did you find out?"

Rob sat down on the corner of the desk. "The forensics team found two different types of DNA on the bedsheets. One was male, taken from a pair of sweaty palm prints they found on the sheets, and the other was Sable's. The blood was hers, and the fingerprints on the IV tubing was hers as well."

Ian turned to Sam. Sam handed him the background report on Sable. "That only tells us that she doesn't have a criminal record. My partner in New Orleans is running down Paul Moran and Nick Granger. By the way, Paul Moran was a victim of identify theft. His name was red flagged three weeks ago."

Cole stepped forward. "I ran DMV photos of Nick Granger and Paul Moran. As you can see, neither of them looks anything like me. I think we need to speak to Jerry Springs again."

Ian looked at the photos and nodded. "Take this with you." He handed the photos back to Cole.

They were interrupted by a deputy. "Excuse me sir, but there is a Callie St. Marie here, and she wants to speak to Rob or Sam."

Ian nodded and turned to Rob. "Who is Callie St. Marie?"

"She's a friend of Sable's who may have the piece of evidence we need to finally see what our killer looks like. I'll be right back." Rob left the room to retrieve the tape.

"Callie stopped by the hospital this morning to see Sable when we were there. She had a CD of a video she took the night Sable went missing," Sam told Ian. "She is also supposed to bring in a list of Sable's friends and family."

Rob returned a few minutes later with a copy of the video. He popped the CD in the computer in the office, and they all watched the footage of Sable dancing in the streets. The scene showed a host of people celebrating. They were singing and dancing and having a great time as they made their way from one street to another. When it didn't reveal what they expected to see, everyone in the room was disappointed.

"If our killer was there, I sure didn't see him," Rob said.

"I sure didn't see anything out of the ordinary. All I saw was a bunch of people having a good time," Ian commented. "What about that list of friends and family? Is there anything on there we can use?"

Sam was quiet for a moment. He felt they had missed something, but he couldn't put his finger on it. "I'm going to check the fax for my reports." As he left the room, he frowned at Cole. Cole's expression confused him—he looked almost relieved. His expression only reaffirmed Sam's suspicions that the agent was hiding something about this killer from the rest of the group.

Just then, Sam heard the phone in Ian's office ring. When he heard Ian swear, he returned to the office. Ian, Rob, and Cole looked furious. "What's happened?" Sam asked.

Ian scowled. "The boat patrol went back to the last sighting of the houseboat to bring in whoever was on board for questioning, and the blasted boat was gone."

Chapter Four

Now what do we do?" asked Cole. "We were so close to nabbing him."

"I'll tell you what we can't do. We can't give up," Sam told them. "If we got that close once, next time he won't get away. He can't have gone very far—there hasn't been enough time."

"What happens if there is no next time?" Rob asked. "What happens if this was the only chance we had?"

"Well, I, for one, am not giving up so easily. That creep turned my life upside down when he murdered my wife, and I want him to pay for that. He left my son without the most important person in his life," grumbled Sam. "Besides, he's already made one mistake. His latest victim got away, and through her, we at least know what he looks like and how he gets around. I can't see this killer letting her live too much longer. We have to find her before he does."

"That's true, but that same victim is now missing, and we don't know for sure if he's got her or if she left on her own," Ian pointed out. He tried to overlook Sam's last statement, but in all conscience couldn't. It sounded very much like Sam wanted this killer for personal reasons. He had to know what his intentions really were. "I've been told you would do your best to bring this killer in to stand trial, but it doesn't sound like you can do that. It sounds more like you are going after him for revenge."

Sam nodded. "It might sound like it, and I don't blame you for thinking that, but I know I can't get my old life back. My wife is gone, and nothing I do is going to bring her back, so all I have left is making sure the man responsible spends the rest of his miserable life in jail."

Ian stared at him for a long moment and nodded. Before he could comment, the phone rang again. Ian answered it. He listened for a moment, and then hung up, his face grim. "That was the hospital. Someone found Sable Willows a little while ago."

"Where was she?" Cole asked.

"A park patrolman found her hiding in a playhouse not too far from the hospital. She had passed out again from loss of blood. She'd ripped open the stitches on her side."

"Did she say anything about why she left the hospital?" Sam asked.

Ian shook his head. "The doctor told me that she was babbling incoherently about not getting away from him, and that he told her he would always be able to find her. He didn't know what that meant, but I think we do."

Everyone turned and looked at Cole. Whether they liked it or not, the evidence was pointing right to him. Cole just stared back at them with a cold look on his face.

Sam headed for the door, but Ian called him back. "The doctor in charge lists her condition as critical. They've put her on life support and have her sedated. No one can talk to her right now."

Everyone was quiet for a moment, and then Rob told his boss, "I'm going over to the hospital. We made a critical error before by not giving her protection, and the killer got to her. That won't happen again, not on my watch."

Ian nodded. "Take a uniformed officer with you. I don't want anyone getting to her." Ian reached for the phone. "I'll call the boat patrol and tell them to search every avenue and backwater branch they can find. I'm not giving up. The boat has to be somewhere."

Sam returned to the desk he'd been using and reached for the phone to call Alec. Maybe if the killer had left this area, he'd gone back to New Orleans. Alec could be looking down there.

"Hunter," Alec answered.

"Alec, we have a problem," Sam told him.

"I was just going to call you. You have a problem on this end too. But first tell me what's happening up there."

"I told you earlier that the killer has been getting around by boat—actually, it's a houseboat. Anyway, the boat patrol up here found it, then temporarily lost sight of it, so we think the killer is tipped off that we know his mode of transportation. Captain Nevell has them looking up and down the river and in all the backwater areas right now, but I wanted you to be looking for the boat down there as well."

"That makes sense. He might have come back down here, especially if he wants you to follow him," Alec said while he wrote down a description of the boat.

"What are you talking about?" Sam asked.

"Before we get into that little surprise, I need to let you know what I found out when I paid Paul Moran a visit. I didn't find Mr. Moran, but I did find a trashed house and blood everywhere. He hasn't been at work, and no one knows where he could be. His family is worried and filed a missing person report last week."

"Why didn't that show up in his background check?" Sam wondered out loud.

"I don't know, but I'm betting that when I get down to Myrtle Grove, I won't find Nick Granger either," Alec surmised.

"Yeah, well, let me know how that goes. What did you mean when you said the killer wants me to follow him?" Sam asked.

"A letter came for you at the station this morning. The words were cut out of several magazines and pasted on paper."

"If it was addressed to me, why did you open it?"

Alec hesitated a moment, wondering just how much he should tell him. "It had a dark stain on the front."

"What kind of dark stain?" Sam asked, already knowing the answer.

"A bloodstain."

"Whose blood?" Sam asked quietly.

"It matched Chloe's blood type."

Sam felt a devastating blow to his heart. For a moment he couldn't speak. Finally, he asked, "What did the letter say?"

"He wants to see if you can find him before he kills again," Alec told him.

Sam was silent for a minute. "What were his exact words?"

"The entire letter reads, 'Can you come out to play a little game of hide-and-seek? The rules are you have to find me before I find another Chloe. That's the only rule.' Pretty sick, if you ask me," Alec said.

Sam knew his partner, and he knew when his partner was holding something back. "What else was in the envelope?"

Alec took a deep breath. "There was a lock of Chloe's hair and a picture of her." Alec paused and then asked, "How did you know there would be something else in the envelope?"

Sam didn't speak for a minute. "Because I'm beginning to know this creep. He would want to make it worth my while to keep coming after him."

"And did he? I mean, did he offer you just enough for you to go after him?"

"He did that when he murdered my wife," Sam said. "Alec, I want you to look after Wyatt and Tessa. This killer won't hesitate to go after them if I don't play his little game, and I don't want them anywhere near him."

"Have you found your witness yet?"

"Yeah, somebody found her, and she's back in the hospital under guard. She may not make it this time, though."

"That's too bad. I was hoping she would make it. I'll move Tessa and Wyatt to a safe house and run down Nick Granger. If I find out anything, I'll let you know. If you need anything, call me," Alec said, ending the call.

Sam stared at the phone for a minute, and then got up to inform Ian of the exchange. Ian wasn't happy with the news. "He's making this personal, isn't he?" Ian looked at Sam. "And he's aiming his sights right on you. Why is that, do you suppose?"

Sam nodded. "I think he wanted it this way from the beginning. The real question is why. What did I do to deserve this honor?"

"Because you were very close to discovering who he really is," came Cole's voice from the doorway.

Sam turned to look at Cole. "What do you mean?"

"You were getting too close to him, and he had to find a way to stop you before you could stop him. I think that's why he killed your wife," Cole told them.

"And just what are you basing your conclusion on?" Sam asked.

"In the four years I've been working this case, I've followed hundreds of leads that didn't turn out. They led nowhere. This killer is very clever that way. But you found out something he doesn't want anyone to know, something he feels will lead the police right to him. He sees you as a threat. So he killed your wife in an attempt to get you as far away from the case as possible."

"He doesn't really know me that well then, does he?" Sam stated. "By killing Chloe, he made sure I would follow him. This won't be over until I see him in prison or he kills me too."

Cole nodded. "He miscalculated the strength of your resolve, but he also knows that your jurisdiction is limited. If he takes himself out of Louisiana, what are you going to do?"

Sam thought for a moment. He hadn't really planned that far ahead. The rage he'd felt at the cemetery was still inside him. He felt it every waking moment. "If he wants to play hide-and-seek with me, he'd better pick a good hiding spot. The game is about to get very rough."

"At what cost?" Cole asked.

"What do you mean?" Sam sensed a threat in the veiled question.

"How far are you willing to go to get this guy off the street?"

"Do you mean, am I willing to kill him before he can kill someone else? Yes, without hesitating, and I wouldn't lose a wink of sleep over it either," Sam stated.

"What are you going to do if he goes after what's left of your family?" Cole asked, still playing the devil's advocate. He knew he was pushing, but he had to know just how far Sam would go.

"My family is protected," Sam assured him. He didn't tell the FBI agent any more than that. He still wasn't one hundred percent sure about Cole, and Sam decided to be safe rather than risk his son's life.

"I hope so, because if he's cornered, he may lash out at the one person he feels is responsible, and that would be you," Cole warned.

Ian could feel the tension escalating between the two men. "Look, we still have to find this creep. I suggest you save the speculation until we do."

Cole looked over at Ian and nodded. Sam didn't say a word. He just left the room. On his way out, he picked up the CD Callie had dropped off that morning and decided to watch it again. He was still sure there was something that they had missed.

Two hours later, he sat up in his chair and grabbed the mouse. He started the file over. This time he was looking for something specific. As he neared the spot he thought he'd seen it, he sat closer to the screen.

He sat back and smiled as he froze the frame. They had missed it earlier. Pointing his finger at the screen like a gun, he shot at the still picture. "Got you, sucker," he told the screen.

Sam grinned as he printed the screenshot. He had his first real piece of evidence that showed the killer's face. When the picture came out of the printer, Sam took it and the disk; he wasn't going to let it out of his possession. He didn't want anyone misplacing it.

He'd been so busy that he had lost track of time. When he left his makeshift office, the station house was almost empty. He looked toward the window and found that it was dark outside. He found a note Cole had left saying he was going back to the motel, so Sam decided to call the hospital to check on Sable.

A few minutes later he was on his way to the motel. Kelly, the night nurse at the hospital, had told him that Sable was doing as well as could be expected. The doctors were keeping her sedated. She told him that the guard was still in place and that Rob had gone home already.

Sam realized that he too was tired. This emotional roller coaster had worn him out. He felt good about the picture, though; at least they had some idea what the killer looked like. But that too brought a problem. What would Cole say when he saw it?

When he pulled into the motel's parking lot, he found a spot next to Cole's sedan. His old blue Pontiac looked rather shabby next to the dark sedan, but Sam didn't care. Chloe had loved his old blue car. Sam smiled as the memories trickled into his brain. He stopped them before the pain of her loss could filter in, and he made his way to his room.

As he opened the door, he saw a letter on the floor just inside the room. Setting his things on the table, he picked up the letter and snapped on the light. He didn't recognize the handwriting, but the letter bore his name. Sitting down on the edge of the bed, he opened the letter.

After reading it, Sam swore and got up. Marching over to the door between his and Cole's room, he banged on it. When a sleepy Cole opened the door, Sam glared at him.

"Did you see anyone outside my room tonight?"

Cole frowned. "No, I didn't, but I've been asleep for a while. Why? Has something else happened?"

"You could say that. The killer left me a note." Sam watched for his reaction.

Cole's eyes widened. "What?" He looked stunned.

Sam cleared his throat in disappointment and turned to grab the phone in his room. He was dialing Rob's number when Cole came into his room. Cole put on a shirt and Sam handed him the letter to read.

When Rob picked up the phone, Sam didn't even bother to say hello. "Rob, the killer left us a little surprise tonight. When I got to my motel room, I found a letter shoved under the door."

"What does it say?"

"Oh, just that he's very upset with us. It seems he thinks we've somehow ruined his plans, and now he tells me that because of us, he had to leave town before he was finished."

"Oh, well, isn't that too bad?" Rob asked sarcastically.

"Yeah, well, I'm a little worried about where this guy is going," Sam told him, "or if this is just a ruse to make us think he's gone." Sam contemplated all the scenarios he could think of. "How is it that he seems to know everything about what we're doing?" Sam speculated out loud. His suspicions about Cole's involvement were resurfacing.

"What are you suggesting? That he has someone on the inside telling him what we're doing?"

"I didn't say that, but as long as you brought it up . . . is that possible?"

"Anything is possible, but the probability is slim," Rob told him.

Sam was looking at Cole and wondering just how he fit into all of this. "Maybe," he told Rob. "I have something to show you in the morning."

"Do you want me to come over now?"

"No, one of us needs to get some sleep. I'll meet you at the station in the morning."

When Sam hung up the phone, Cole turned and handed him back the letter. "I've been here since seven," Cole said. They both looked at the clock on the wall. It read 11:00 P.M. "I didn't notice anything, and I didn't hear anything. I haven't been sleeping very well, so I took a sleeping pill and it put me right out. I'm sorry."

Sam didn't know if he should believe him or not. Was it just another coincidence that the killer had come here with Cole right next door, or was there more to it than that? And why did Cole take a sleeping pill tonight of all nights?

"I think, for my own safety, I should get a room somewhere else for as long as I'm here. I don't want to wake up one morning with my throat cut," Sam told him without any further reason.

Cole nodded. "I'll see you in the morning, then." He walked back through the connecting door and closed it behind him. Sam walked over to it and turned the lock on his side of the door. He wasn't taking any chances.

Sam sat on the bed again. All thoughts of getting any sleep tonight were gone. He knew his body was running on empty, but his mind wouldn't let him rest. He picked up the letter again and reread it.

It was like the letter that Alec said was delivered to him in New Orleans. The words were cut from magazines and pasted on the paper. Sam frowned as he read it a third time. There was something odd about a few of the letters—they were capitalized for no reason. He grabbed a pen and spelled out a sentence with the capital letters. He finished and read what he'd written. The message read SABLE WILL DIE TONIGHT.

Chapter Five

Sam grabbed his keys and headed out the door. He was going to the hospital to check on Sable. As he got into his car, he noticed something odd about Cole's car. He couldn't immediately register what was different, but something definitely was. He didn't have time to investigate, however; he needed to check on Sable. He got into his car and started driving to the hospital. Even at this late hour, there was enough traffic to slow him down. Patience wasn't one of his virtues when he had somewhere to be. Sam's fingers tapped the steering wheel.

He pulled into the parking lot and rushed inside. The halls of the hospital were quiet and empty as he made his way to the second floor. Taking two steps at a time, his footsteps echoed in the stairwell. He cautiously opened the door to the second floor. Looking up and down the corridor, he didn't notice anything amiss. When he got to Sable's room, he didn't see a guard outside her door.

Sam frowned and drew his weapon. Flattening himself against the wall, he peeked inside the room. He could see Sable lying on the bed, and there didn't seem to be anything wrong. He put his gun away and opened the door. He saw a crack of light coming from under the bathroom door. Thinking that the guard was using the facilities, Sam approached the bed.

Sam's head exploded in pain as something hard came down on the back of his head. He dropped to the floor, unconscious.

The shadowy figure dragged Sam out of sight of the window and smiled.

He had accomplished what he had set out to do. The only witness that could identify him was dead, and he got a bonus. The cop who had tried to destroy him was lying at his mercy. The man squatted down beside the unconscious Sam. Thoughts of slitting Sam's throat entered his mind, but he thought that would end the game too soon, and he had other plans for Sam.

The rivalry between Sam Sebastian and himself made the game more interesting. He hadn't yet come across a better opponent, and over the years a few good men had challenged him. Then he got another idea. He could leave Sam with a permanent reminder of his brush with death. His black eyes sparkled with merriment as he reached for the front of Sam's shirt.

He ripped open Sam's shirt and exposed his chest. Reaching for the knife that was never far, the man began twisting the handle to expose a secret compartment. From it he took out a special surgeon's scalpel and began to carve the design he was infamous for. Sam moaned a little—a sound he relished as long as his rival remained unconscious. He couldn't make his design as elaborate as he would have liked, or as deep—after all, he didn't want Sam to bleed to death. No, he wanted Sam to be able to finish the game. When he was done he sat back and looked at his creation. It would do.

Leaving Sam alive, the killer got up and looked out the window of the door. The halls were empty, and he knew he had better make his escape while he could. He certainly didn't want to get caught now. Slipping through the door, he made his way undetected through the hospital corridor and down the stairs. Once outside, he blended with the shadows of the night.

A few hours later, as the sun was peeking over the horizon, Rob walked up to the front entrance of the hospital. Yawning, he pulled open the doors and entered the establishment. While he waited for the elevator, his cell phone rang. It was the hospital calling. He frowned. Rob listened for a moment and then swore. He shoved the phone back in his pocket and raced to the stairs. He rushed up to the second floor. He pushed open the door and ran down the hall to Sable's room.

He stopped when he saw hospital personnel working on a figure on the floor. Glancing over the doctor's shoulder, he saw that the man on the floor was Sam. The doctors were trying to stop the bleeding on his chest. Rob looked over at the bed and found a sheet covering Sable's body. The sheet bore several large bloodstains. Rob looked around for the guard who should have been outside the room last night. The door to the bathroom was open, revealing his body lying on the floor. The pool of blood around his neck told its own story.

"What the hell happened here?" Rob demanded.

A doctor looked up from the work he was doing on Sam's chest. His name badge read DR. JOHN ROSS. He glared at Rob. "What the hell does it look like happened here? It certainly wasn't a picnic."

Rob looked at Sam. "Is he going to make it?"

Dr. Ross nodded. "He's the only one out of the three who will. The other two are already dead. Your killer only cut him superficially. He's going to have a rather unique scar though."

Rob stepped over to Sam's body and examined the killer's handiwork. He winced as he studied the design the killer had carved into Sam's chest. All he could make out was a bunch of squiggles and lines. To Rob, the design didn't make any sense.

Sam groaned as he began to wake up. His chest felt as if it was on fire, and his head hurt like hell. He tried to open his eyes, but the light blinded him. For a moment, he didn't remember where he was. Then he heard a voice calling his name. He tried again to open his eyes. The first thing he saw was a doctor's face, and beyond him stood Rob. Rob was looking a little grey around the edges, and Sam had to ask, "What's going on?"

When he remembered, he tried to sit up. The doctor introduced himself, placed a hand on his chest, and told him to lie still. Dr. Ross finished taping the gauge on his chest and assisted Sam in sitting up.

Sam's chest and head hurt. For a moment he couldn't stand the pain, but it lessened after a few minutes. Holding his chest, Sam looked over toward the bed. "Is she dead?" he asked Rob.

Rob nodded. "Both she and the cop who was guarding her are dead. What happened here?"

Sam reached for Rob's hand to help him to his feet. Dr. Ross grabbed the chair and told him to sit down. As Sam sat in the chair, he began telling his story. "I took another look at the note the killer left after our phone call. There was something odd about the way some of the letters were positioned, so I grabbed a pen and figured out that the killer left a message within the letter. It said that Sable was going to die tonight. I came over here hoping to prevent that from happening. Man, I didn't see anything," Sam groaned. "I was walking toward the bed when he hit me from behind."

"Did you see the cop that was supposed to be on guard?" Rob asked.

"No, I thought he was using the bathroom," Sam told them.

"The killer dragged him in there and let him bleed to death from a cut on his throat," Dr. Ross informed them.

Sam looked toward the bed. "What about Sable?"

Dr. Ross nodded toward her body covered by the bloody sheet. "He must have heard someone coming. He slit her throat as well. You probably didn't see it at first, coming from the door. The cut is on the other side of her neck. She bled out quickly, and more than likely didn't even know it was happening. She's been heavily sedated."

Sam remembered something else. His eyes widened as he recalled the strange appearance of Cole's car. "Rob, you have to warn Cole. I thought I saw something moving in his car last night when I got into my car to come here. I didn't know what it was, exactly, but something inside seemed to be alive. Call him and tell him to check his car over really well before he gets into it."

Rob nodded and reached for his phone to call Cole. He didn't like the way this case was going. If this killer was bold enough to murder a cop in as public a place as a hospital, there might not be a way to stop him.

When Rob finished his call to Cole, he turned to find Sam arguing with Dr. Ross. "What's the problem?" Rob asked.

Sam turned his glare on Rob. "The good doctor is insisting that I stay, and I don't want to."

Dr. Ross rolled his eyes toward the ceiling. "You've lost quite a bit of blood, and you probably have a mild concussion. You need to be where someone can keep an eye on you."

Sam made a face at Rob that told him to get him out of the situation. Rob chuckled under his breath and then, clearing his throat, said, "Doc, how about if we promise that if we notice any change for the worse, or we'll bring him right back?"

Dr. Ross wasn't happy about what they were suggesting, but he knew if he pushed it Sam probably wouldn't come back at all. "Stop back after you get done for the day and have that bandage changed. If it starts to bleed again, you need to get medical attention right away. You also need to rest at least part of the day."

After the physician left the room, Sam told Rob, "I don't think he cared too much for letting me go, but thanks for your help. What did Cole say?"

Rob shook his head. "Cole is very grateful to you. He was about to reach for his door handle when he got the call. He looked inside the car and found a snake curled up in the driver's seat—and not just any snake, but a cottonmouth. It's a rather nasty creature, found in the backwater areas and, by the way, very poisonous."

"Our killer is getting braver. By killing Sable he may be telling us that he's ready to move on to another place," Sam wondered aloud.

"Maybe he got rid of his witness so he could concentrate on you," Rob suggested.

"Speaking of the killer, I went back to the CD Callie brought in, and I found out what he looks like."

"What did you say?" Rob frowned.

"I said I know what our killer looks like, and I think Cole Davidson has some questions to answer," Sam said.

"Cole? What does he have to do with this?"

"Let's go back to the station and ask him, shall we? Maybe Alec will have called back. I asked him to check on Nick Granger yesterday. I need to talk to him anyway. I need to know that what's left of my family is safe. If this killer is after me, he might go after them out of spite," Sam concluded.

Rob helped him stand and assisted him out of the hospital and into Sam's car. He drove them both to the station house. Rob could tell that Sam wasn't up to working, but he was just stubborn enough not to give in to his pain. Before they got out of Sam's car, Sam reached into the glove compartment for the CD and photo from the night before. In his jacket pocket was the letter the killer had left for him.

Ian and Cole were waiting for them inside. Rob assisted Sam into Ian's office and helped ease him onto the sofa. Ian took one look at Sam and almost ordered Rob to take him back to the hospital. He held his tongue when Rob shook his head behind Sam's back.

Sam had to close his eyes for a moment once he was settled. He almost asked Rob to take him home, but he knew he couldn't give in to the pain.

Sam opened his eyes and focused his energy on the case they were working. "The killer left me a note last night. I found it on the floor of my room." He took the note out of his pocket and handed it over to Rob. "See how the capital letters form the message within the letter."

Rob, Ian and Cole read the letter and the message the killer had left. Ian nodded and then picked up another letter the killer had left for Sam. "Your partner Alec faxed this letter to us this morning. He said he talked to you about it yesterday and thought you might want to see the actual letter."

Sam took the letter from Ian and looked it over carefully. The killer had left a message in this letter as well.

Sam grabbed a pen and began writing. When he was finished he reread the message. He swore and handed the message to Ian.

Ian read the message and handed it to Rob and Cole. He looked at Sam and asked, "What are you going to do now?"

Sam looked at him. "I don't have a choice."

Rob looked again at the words Sam had written on the bottom of the letter: I HAVE YOUR SON.

"I think he's bluffing," Rob told them. "You said it yourself—Alec took them to a safe house."

Sam nodded. "That's right. I'd forgotten about that." He reached for his cell phone and dialed Alec's number. Alec answered on the third ring. "Alec, please tell me Wyatt and Tessa are safe."

"Hello to you too," Alec said. "As far as I know they're fine, but if you want, I'll call and check on them."

"You do that. Thanks for sending the fax of the letter you got at the station, by the way. Did you know there was a secret message in it? I got another letter last night, shoved under my motel room door. Something in it looked odd, and I realized I had found a hidden message." Sam tried to explain. He paused a moment and then told Alec, "He got to our witness. She's dead, and so is the cop who was guarding her. He almost got me as well, but instead of killing me he carved one of his designs in my chest."

"Are you all right?" Alec asked.

"Oh, I'll live, but I need you to check on Wyatt and Tessa and get back to me right away. Be careful. If he knows you're going to check on them, he might follow you," Sam warned.

"What was the message in the letter I faxed you?" Alex asked.

"Just go and check on Wyatt and Tessa for me," Sam replied. "I need to know they are okay."

"I'll be careful," Alec assured Sam. "I'll call you back in a few minutes."

The next fifteen minutes seemed to take forever. Everyone waited for the phone call in silence. Finally, Sam's cell phone began to ring. In his hurry to answer it, Sam almost dropped the phone. "Well, are they okay?" he asked.

"Sam, I don't know what to say." Alec didn't know how to tell him what had happened. Wyatt was missing; Tessa and the two cops guarding them were dead. "He's gone."

Chapter Six

Wat do you mean, he's gone?" Sam demanded.
"Gone as in missing, or gone as in he's dead?" He could
barely speak as he waited for the fateful news.

"I'm sorry, he's missing," Alec clarified. "Tessa and
two cops are dead. Wyatt is missing. There were signs
of a struggle, so whatever went down, your killer didn't
just walk in there and snatch the boy."

"How could you let this happen? You told me you
were going to take them to a safe house."

"How the hell do I know how it happened?" Alec exploded. "I did take him to a safe house. I personally
picked out two of the best cops I knew to watch over
your son and your mother-in-law. I even went over there
and had supper with them last night after work." Alec
paused to catch his breath. "He must have followed me
over there."

"He must have left here in time to follow you over to
the safe house. Then he came back here to finish off

Sable and went back to kidnap Wyatt," Sam reasoned. "Man, he didn't sleep at all."

Alec was quiet for a moment. Then he said, "I assumed this creep was in or around Baton Rouge. I wasn't expecting him to be anywhere near here. He got to your son because I was sloppy. I'm sorry. I screwed up, and now I have to tell Sally Carter and Meg Keller that their husbands won't be coming home."

Sam felt a moment of regret for his friends. "I'm sorry, man, but a killer has my son."

"I'm sorry too. I didn't mean to blow up at you. What can I do to help?" Alec asked.

"Did you find Nick Granger?" Sam asked.

"He is on the missing list, but his neighbors aren't too worried. He's often gone for weeks at a time. There's still no word on Paul Moran. What are you going to do about Wyatt?" Alec asked.

"I don't know. I'm sure I'll hear from him again. I'll let you know when I find something out." Sam ended the call. He looked at the others. "That monster has my son. He's killed my mother-in-law and two cops Alec sent to watch over them."

"You said earlier that you found out what he looked like from Callie's CD," Rob reminded him. He wasn't trying to distract Sam, but they needed to know who or what to look for.

Sam nodded. "Yeah, I know what he looks like. Didn't you find it odd that three strangers all claimed that they knew you, Cole? I know I did." Sam picked up the CD and the photo from the sofa beside him. Handing the photo to Rob, he waited for their reaction.

Rob looked at the photo, then handed it to Ian. Ian looked at it and handed it to Cole. After Cole viewed the damning photo, he looked at the other three. "This is not a photo of me."

They all saw the similarities, yet there were subtle differences. Both men had the same square face shape, but the man in the photo had a scar above his left eyebrow, and his eyes looked cold and dead.

"Do you have a twin brother?" Rob asked.

"No, I'm an only child," Cole stated. He sighed heavily, and finally he knew he had to admit what he'd been trying so hard to hide. "But I do have a first cousin who is often mistaken for my twin."

"Excuse me?" Ian interjected. He was astonished by this news. Cole had known this killer all along.

Sam made a low growling sound in his throat and looked as if he was ready to spring at the other man. Rob had to put his hand on Sam's shoulder to stop him. When Sam glared at Rob, Rob just shook his head. "Give him a chance to explain before you punch him."

"It's complicated, so bear with me." Cole ran his hands through his hair while he considered what he would tell them about his family. He knew what he was about to say wouldn't look good in any light, but he had to try to make them understand. "My father has an identical twin brother, Ethan. They married identical twin sisters, Emily and Joyce. My parents had me, and Ethan and Joyce had a son they called Tucker. We were born in the same month about three weeks apart. I'm the younger one. Tucker and I look very similar and have always been mistaken for twins."

"So the killer has a name, Tucker Davidson," Sam murmured as the rage inside him grew.

"He prefers to be called Tucker Briggs," Cole told them.

"Why?" Rob asked. He looked at the photo again and found the resemblance a little unnerving.

Cole sighed again. "Twins do everything together. They work together, play together, eat together—they even sometimes think together. Our two families were like that. Tucker and I weren't twins, but that somehow escaped our parents. When Tucker started going out of his way to stress his individuality, they didn't know how to deal with him, so they ignored him until he became a problem."

"What kind of problem?" Ian asked.

"When he was a boy he would cause trouble just to get his parents' attention. Just little things, mind you, but it was enough to get attention focused on just him. When he got a little older, he began setting small fires. No one really got hurt, and the fires were never out of control, but he was." Cole paused in his story.

"What changed that turned him from a prankster to a killer?" Sam asked, already fearing the worst.

"Ethan and Joyce had another baby. Tucker was about fifteen when his mother got pregnant. This time they were going to have a set of twins. Everyone was so excited about the babies that they forgot all about Tucker's little problem. Things got really bad there for a while."

"What pushed him over the edge? What made him a killer?" Sam demanded.

Cole dreaded telling them this part of the story. "Like I said, we were fifteen, and we were in chemistry class when one of the school's big mouths, a guy named John Orland, found out about the twins due to be born any day. He started teasing Tucker about having a reason now for his being such a wimp, and that he would have to be sure and teach the new babies how to follow in their big brother's footsteps." Cole ran his fingers through his hair again. "You have to understand something. When Tucker found out that the babies were coming, he was furious. His sense of self deteriorated after that. He felt invisible, and John's words pounded that home. Tucker looked to me for help against John, and I just pretended I didn't hear what was being said. Shoot, John had half the school afraid to walk on the same side of the hall as him. Tucker and I were only fifteen."

"What happened?" Rob asked.

"Tucker went over to his chemistry lab table and began mixing chemicals together while the teacher was giving us our assignment. I was his partner, but I wasn't paying attention to what he was doing, I was listening to the teacher. The next thing I knew, Tucker walked over to where John was sitting and threw a formula in his face. I don't think I've ever heard anyone scream the way John did that day. Whatever Tucker had mixed up had done the trick. The solution burned John's face so badly that he ended up in the hospital. He barely survived the attack."

"Is he alive today?" Ian asked.

Cole shook his head. "No, he couldn't live with the way his face looked after the solution was washed away. It took most of his face. John ended up committing suicide a year or so later."

"What happened to Tucker?" Sam asked.

"Rather than go to jail for assault, he ran away. Our parents tried to find him, but when Tucker makes up his mind about something, he doesn't often change it. He felt he had no place at home, and the only time I've spoken to him since then, he made it very clear that he wasn't coming back."

"What tipped you off that he might be the killer?" Ian asked.

Cole took a deep breath. "It was the design he left on his victims. When I was about seven or eight, I had a dog. When he died, Tucker and I were devastated. Tucker sat down the day we buried the dog and drew the design for the headstone. It was so cool back then. We had his dad burn it onto a piece of wood we used to mark where the dog was buried.

"Now he uses that same design to mark the people he kills," Cole stated.

"I don't get it. As far as I can tell there's no set pattern—it's all a bunch of lines and squiggles," Rob said.

Cole shook his head. "You don't know what you're looking at. Look, I'll show you." He went over to his briefcase and pulled out one of the photos inside. Then he went over to the one-way glass and held up the picture. The reflection on the glass showed exactly what Rob said it would: a bunch of squiggly lines and curves. Cole reached for a marker and began connecting the lines.

The pattern that began to emerge showed a headstone of sorts with a name inside. The name was Paula. She was one of his first victims. So not only did he torture his victims, but he marked each one with their own headstone.

"Why wasn't this information ever revealed? Why did you keep it a secret?" Ian demanded. He didn't know what he was going to do about this latest turn of events. It seemed that both men had a personal reason for hunting this killer, and that could be either an advantage or a disadvantage. Ian knew that Cole's story didn't show him in a good light, but his willingness to try to stop his cousin could. They would have to wait and see what developed next. He glanced over at Sam and saw the hatred in his eyes. Ian had to wonder if the hatred was for Cole or for his cousin Tucker.

Cole laid the photo on Ian's desk. "I kept hoping that I would be the one to find him. If I could, then maybe I could get him the help he needs. He is still family."

"He has my six-year-old son. Will he kill a child?" Sam asked.

"He hasn't yet, but I don't know what he's capable of anymore." Cole spoke frankly. He needed to gain back the trust his story and his connection to the killer had lost.

"Does anyone in the FBI know about your connection with this killer?" Ian asked.

Cole nodded. "My boss, Clayton Conway, knows. I had to tell him when I figured out it was Tucker we were looking for. He was going to pull me off the case, but I told him I was the only one who could find him. I told him we grew up together and that no one knew him better than I did. Clayton agreed to my staying on the case, but he told me that he was going to watch me closely. He insisted that I check in with him on a regular basis."

Ian nodded and stared at Cole. "As long as your intent is to stop him, not assist him, I'll hold off on passing judgment, but now you've got two people watching your every move. If I have any concerns about either of you, I will yank you both off the case."

Ian reached for the phone. "I'm calling the boat patrol to see if they've found anything yet. Maybe we'll get lucky."

As the morning slid into afternoon and there was still no word about Wyatt, Sam felt as if he was going crazy. He still felt very weak, and he drifted in and out of sleep. He wanted to be out on the street pounding on doors, at least making an effort to find his son. Instead he was stuck in the station, waiting for news. He had already decided that the waiting was the worst. As a cop, he could handle the searching, because he knew that maybe around the next corner he might find what he was looking for. But waiting while others searched was enough to drive him insane.

Alec had called back, and Sam had had nothing new to tell him. Sam asked Alec to send him the rest of the files they had on this killer. As long as he had to wait, he figured he might as well do something. The files had been e-mailed a couple of hours before, and Sam was already going through them. He had printed out the documents and photos so the monitor wouldn't strain his eyes.

He was on the Robin Myron case. The first two cases hadn't really told him anything new, or at least he wasn't seeing anything new. When he opened the Myron case, though, a photo fell out. Sam reached down to pick it up and had to stop to catch his breath. The picture was of his wife. It had been snapped at the Fourth of July picnic just two weeks before her death.

Chloe was sitting on the merry-go-round in the park near their home. She looked so relaxed and carefree, and the love for him in her eyes slammed his heart, crushing his senses.

How the photograph of Chloe ended up in the Myron file, Sam didn't know. He suddenly sat up. He remembered something. Sam had taken the photo the day they had found the body of Sandy Danvers. He had been in the park with Chloe and Wyatt having a picnic when someone had come running up to him. A body had been found, and everyone in the area knew he was a cop.

He had called it in to the precinct, and while they

were waiting for the Crime Scene Unit to get there, Sam began snapping pictures of the crime scene. It was clouding up and even a shower could wash away evidence. Sure enough, the rain came just as he finished shooting the photos. His photos were all the police had of the crime scene. Sam must have shoved Chloe's photo into the Myron file by mistake.

Sam didn't know why, but he needed to see the rest of the photos he took that day. He reached for the phone and called Alec.

Alec answered on the first ring. "Hunter."

"Alec, this is Sam."

"Has there been any word on Wyatt?" Alec asked.

"No, nothing yet—I only wish there were. I want him back with me. I called to ask you to send the photos from the Sandy Danvers file."

"Why? What does Sandy Danvers have to do with the killer?"

"I don't know, maybe nothing, but when I opened the Robin Myron case file, a picture of Chloe fell out. I remembered that it was the day of the picnic that we found Sandy's body. CSU couldn't get to the crime scene before the rain, and I ended up taking the photos. A victim of Tucker's was found nearby just three days afterward. Maybe there is something in the photos that will link the two crimes. It's a long shot, but right now it's all I've got," Sam told him.

"I'll e-mail those photos to you as fast as I can get the file." He paused and then said, "I hope you know that I would never put your son in any danger. I know I screwed up by not watching for someone following, but I never meant to put Wyatt or anyone else in danger."

Sam didn't hesitate. "I know that, and I was wrong to accuse you earlier. I know you love Wyatt. Blame it on a father's love, or on the fact that I've had a heck of a week and I was in a lot of pain. Don't worry, we'll find him—we have to. I can't imagine anything else. Just e-mail those photos right away."

"I will. And Sam"—Alec paused—"if you get your hands on the creep, kill him. Do not let him go."

Sam snorted. "I don't think escape is even an option. He has a lot to answer for, and when I find him, he'll pay."

Sam went over the Robin Myron case again and again while he waited for the photos from Alec to come in. He had a hunch the two cases were related, but he didn't know how. Sandy Danvers' killer had been her ex-boyfriend Toby Rains. It had been a domestic dispute gone bad. What possible connection that case had with this one escaped him. He'd gone over and over the crime scene photos until he couldn't look at them any-more, and still there was nothing he could find.

Sam got up to check his e-mail. His photos were in his inbox. He printed them out and took them back to his desk and checked over each one carefully. He even looked over the fine details with a magnifying glass. If there was something there, he didn't find it. He threw down the glass in frustration.

Sam took a deep breath and got up to get a drink. A cup of coffee would taste good right now, and he needed the stimulation. He saw Cole just leaving the station and wondered if there was any news on Wyatt yet. Sam turned to check with Ian and found Cole standing in the office door.

Sam was stunned as the realization hit him. Tucker Briggs had just been in the building.

Sam began running, while calling out for the others. He shoved the door open and hit the streets. Looking both ways, he thought he saw the telltale black cowboy hat down the street to his right. Rob, Cole, and Ian were right behind him with their guns drawn.

"What's going on?" Rob asked from two steps behind Sam.

"Tucker Briggs just paid us a visit," Sam told them as he dodged the people on the street. He didn't want to lose sight of the cowboy hat, but the traffic on the street was making it impossible to keep it in his line of vision.

When they got to the corner, Sam looked around again. The cowboy hat was nowhere in sight. Frantically, he looked again, but the hat was gone. "Blast it, where did he go?" Sam grabbed his chest, wincing in pain as he tried to catch his breath.

"Whoa, wait a minute." Ian grabbed his arm. "What did you say before?"

Sam turned and jerked his arm out of Ian's grasp. "I was walking toward the kitchen and I looked up and thought I saw Cole leaving the building. I turned around to go back to your office and I saw Cole standing in your doorway. The Cole I saw leaving could only have been Tucker Briggs, so I gave chase. Now I've lost him again." Then he turned to Cole. "Unless you have another cousin or brother who looks exactly like you and wears a black cowboy hat?"

Cole put his gun away and sighed deeply. "No, that would be Tucker," he said quietly. "I wonder what he was doing at the station."

Rob and Ian put their weapons away as well. "Let's go find out," Rob said. Rob was getting worried. If the man had been Tucker Briggs, he was getting brazen. His appearance at the station house was certainly unexpected.

When they entered the station house, Sam strode up to the front desk and asked the man behind the desk, "Did Cole Davidson leave anything with you just a few minutes ago?"

Officer Larry Paulson nodded and reached behind him for the envelope Cole had just left. Handing it over, he said, "I thought it was strange that he would leave it with me."

Sam pursed his lips. "It wasn't Cole who left it—it was the killer we're after."

Larry looked from Sam to Ian and Rob. Rob just shook his head and followed everyone into Ian's office.

Sam ripped open the letter and began reading it. By the time he finished he was scowling. Handing the letter to Rob, he simply walked away. He was in a dangerous mood right now and didn't want to hurt anyone. He walked back to his temporary desk and glanced down at the photos from the Danvers case. The magnifying glass had fallen just right, and through it he saw a man helping someone into a car. The woman looked as though she was sleeping, but what caught Sam's attention was the black cowboy hat the man was wearing.

Sam grabbed the picture and looked at it again. The man he now knew as Tucker Briggs was standing there as big as life.

Sam turned to go back into the office. His earlier rage was still there, but now he knew why Tucker had zeroed in on him.

"I got the creep. Now I know why he came after me."

"Why?" Cole asked as Sam handed him the photograph.

"I caught him on film at another crime scene. He's helping his next victim into her own car. This picture was taken at a Fourth of July picnic, and three days later we found this woman dead. That was exactly two weeks before he murdered my wife," Sam explained.

"But how would he know that you got his picture?" Cole asked.

"He was at the park when someone discovered a dead body. He could have heard the commotion when someone yelled out to call nine-one-one. I was there at the park that day with my family. I rushed to the scene and announced that I was a cop, and he could have noticed I was taking pictures of everything and anything." Sam shrugged. "Maybe he couldn't take the chance that I hadn't taken his picture that day. I didn't exactly hide the fact I was a cop, and it looked like the skies were going to dump rain on us at any minute. I took those pictures just before it rained. Rain has a way of washing away any evidence that may be there."

Chapter Seven

Give me that letter again," Sam demanded. When Cole handed it to him, Sam reread it, and then looked at the others. "The letter says to go back to the beginning. I wonder if he means go back to where we first met."

"That would be the park where you took his picture," Cole stated.

"I have to be there by midnight." Sam looked at his watch. He had just enough time to make it back to New Orleans before the deadline.

"You can't drive all that way by yourself," Ian told him.

"Why not?"

"In case you haven't noticed, you're bleeding again," Ian pointed out. In the rush to catch Tucker, Sam's chest wound had started leaking. The front of his shirt was stained with fresh blood.

Sam swore as he felt a wave of nausea coming on. He had to sit down quickly. He fell against the sofa in

Ian's office and waited for it to pass. He hated being this weak.

"Let me go," Cole suggested.

Sam shook his head. "No, I won't jeopardize anyone else's life, and I don't want to lose the only chance I may have to get my son back alive." He still didn't trust Cole. For all Sam knew, the cousins could be working together.

"At least let me drive. That way you can rest on the way," Cole offered.

Sam nodded. "Okay, you can drive, but we have to leave now. I don't want to be late." He fished the keys out of his pocket and tossed them to Cole. Looking at Ian and Rob, he told them, "Be careful. This may be a trap."

Rob nodded. "I was about to tell you the same thing." He hesitated a moment. "You do realize that your son might already be dead and that this could be Tucker's way of getting to you as well, don't you? If that's what he has in mind, this time he won't let you live."

Sam thought about the words he'd been too afraid to say out loud. "Yeah, I've thought about it, but he's my son, the only family I have left. If I didn't go, and Tucker killed Wyatt because I wasn't there, I don't think I could live with that. I know how big a chance I'm taking, but I don't really have a choice, do I?"

Rob shook his head. "I see your point. Good luck."

Rob and Ian watched as Sam and Cole left. Ian reached for the phone and called Alec, Sam's partner in New Orleans, and explained the situation to him.

Ian grabbed his coat. "What are you waiting for?" he

asked Rob. "He'll need backup if he's going up against this creep, and I'm not going to wait to hear about it in the morning news."

Rob grinned and grabbed his jacket.

Darkness had long ago fallen by the time Sam and Cole got to their destination. The park was eerily empty as they drove through the gates. They could only drive so far and then they had to walk, but Sam had rested most of the way, so he felt stronger. Pulling into the parking lot, they didn't see any other vehicles. Sam and Cole drew their guns as they got out of the car.

The park had several trails for pedestrians and bikers, and if you didn't know where you were going you could easily get lost. But Sam knew this park. He had asked Chloe to marry him here, and they had brought Wyatt here as a family. Now he was here to catch the man who had murdered his wife and stolen his son.

Sam slowed as they approached the area of the Danvers murder. This was where Sam had snapped the incriminating picture of Tucker Briggs. Sam squatted behind a bush and dragged Cole down behind him. He didn't want to give Tucker a target. He wanted the element of surprise on his side.

His eyes canvassed the entire area. Nothing seemed out of place. The moon was big and bright, and there didn't appear to be anyone around, but that didn't mean that the shadows were empty. He motioned for Cole to stay put. Using the bushes for cover, Sam began making his way around the other side of the trail.

Sam kept a keen eye out for any movement or sign that someone might be nearby. He didn't see or hear anything. He'd almost given up when he heard a twig snap. His head jerked toward the location of the noise. His eyes narrowed and his ears picked up the sound of footsteps coming down the path toward him.

Sam waited with his gun drawn. He could hear the footsteps hesitate. "Hello?" called out a frail voice.

Sam frowned and dared to raise his head over the top of the bush he was hiding behind. An old man stood on the path. He was dirty and had a scruffy beard. His cap had seen better days, as had his clothes. They hung on his frame and were covered in filth. His stance told Sam that he was probably drunk. He could barely stand up straight. Sam noticed the top of a bottle sticking out of his coat pocket.

"I'm looking for Sam. Is there anyone there?" the old man called out again, his words slurred.

Sam stood up and put his gun away. He knew that this could very well be a trap and that Tucker could be hiding nearby, but he wasn't going to pull a gun on a drunk. He stepped out of the bushes and onto the path.

When he cleared his throat the man whirled around and almost fell over. "Geez man, you scared me. Is your name Sam?"

When Sam nodded, the older man smiled. "I have something for you," he told him. Reaching inside his overcoat, the older man pulled out a large manila envelope and handed it to Sam.

Cole saw the exchange and he too put his weapon

away and stepped out from where he'd hidden. When the old man saw Cole, he looked confused. He glanced back the way he had come and then turned back to Cole.

Sam ripped open the envelope and dumped out its contents. There was a picture of Wyatt holding today's newspaper, and another letter. He looked up at the old man. "Who gave you this?"

The old man pointed at Cole. "He did. I was sitting over at the other end of the park, and he walked up to me and gave me the envelope. He told me all I had to do was walk down here and give it to you. He even gave me ten bucks." The old man turned to Cole. "Why would you do that if you were already here? Why didn't you just give it to him yourself?" He frowned as he swayed and stared at Cole. "I ain't giving you the money back."

Cole shook his head. "I don't want it back. Did I say anything else?"

The old man thought for a moment, then shook his head. Cole looked over at Sam. They both knew it wasn't Cole who'd given the old man the package. Tucker had done it again. He had once again become Cole, if only for a moment.

"What does the letter say?" Cole asked.

Sam ripped open the letter. As he read it, he felt himself pale and could see Cole growing alarmed. Sam looked up at Cole. "He says that he's going to keep Wyatt with him a while. He doesn't know for how long, but when he gets tired of him, he'll call me and let me know where to pick him up." Sam looked over at the old man. "Did you see where the man who gave you this letter went?"

The old man nodded and pointed at Cole. "Yep, he's standing right there. Can I go now?"

Sam heard more footsteps coming down the path. He grabbed his gun and turned to face whatever or whoever was coming. When he heard a familiar whistle, he relaxed his stance and called out, "Alec, is that you?"

Alec Hunter, Ian Nevell, and Rob Gillette stepped out of the shadows. Sam raised an eyebrow at the sight of all three of them. As he was putting his gun away, he asked, "To what do I owe this pleasurable reunion?"

Before anyone could answer, the old man asked again, "Can I go?" Sam looked at him and asked, "Where can I find you if I need to get ahold of you?"

The old man smiled. "I'm usually in the park somewhere. I like watching the kids. I don't hurt them or nothing, I just like to watch them play. They all know me. My name is Joe." Joe turned to leave, when he remembered something else. "Say, you should tell that man over there not to leave his son standing by himself like that. Somebody could snatch the kid."

Sam grabbed Joe by his jacket. "What did you say? What kid?"

Joe's eyes grew huge and he held up his hands as if to ward off an attack. "I'm sorry, mister—I didn't mean nothing."

Sam shook his head and took a deep breath as he tried to calm down. He let go of Joe's jacket. "No, I'm sorry. You were just trying to warn me. What did you mean by that warning? Did you see the kid? Where was he standing?" Sam grabbed the picture Tucker had left for him and showed it to Joe. "Is this the kid you saw?"

Joe took the picture from Sam and looked it over. "Yep, that's the kid. He was standing all alone over by the merry-go-round. The man walked away from the kid to find me and was gone for quite a while."

Sam closed his eyes in relief. At least Wyatt was still alive. He knew exactly where the merry-go-round was, and he started running toward it. He heard the others following, but he didn't care. Maybe Tucker had left Wyatt there and he was waiting for Sam to come get him. As Sam turned the corner and saw the merry-go-round, he looked around. Wyatt wasn't there. Crushing disappointment set in. Sam didn't know if he could take this seesawing emotional trip anymore. He fell to his knees, his eyes burning with unshed tears.

From the darkness, hidden in the shadows of the night, a pair of black eyes watched as Sam fell to the ground. Tucker Briggs smiled as he watched the torment of the man he'd chosen to play the game with. The boy at his feet struggled to break free of his bonds and escape, but Tucker pulled him to his feet and dragged him through the brush. He wasn't quite done with either the boy or his father, not just yet anyway.

It was Alec who helped Sam up off the ground when the others joined him in front of the merry-go-round. He could see the pain in his partner's eyes and knew what Sam was going through. "Sam, you can't let him win. You have to be strong for Wyatt's sake." Alec tried to brace his friend against the tide of emotion he knew he was facing.

Sam looked at Alec. "I don't know how much more of this I can take. First he took Chloe, and now he has Wyatt. Why doesn't he just kill me and get it over with?"

Alec was at a loss for words. He didn't know what to say to make it any better. It was Cole who put it in perspective. "If you fold now, you'll never see Wyatt again—not alive, anyway."

Sam and Alec turned to the man who looked so much like the one they both hated. "What the hell is that supposed to mean?" Sam growled.

Cole held up the letter Tucker had left for Sam. "I think I know where he's going," Cole told them. "And if you don't follow him, he might kill Wyatt out of spite. Then you'll never find Wyatt or his body."

Sam stumbled away from Alec toward Cole. "Where? Where is he going?"

Cole straightened his jaw. "I think he's going to a place we played as kids, before all this started. I think he's going home."

"And where exactly is home?" Sam growled.

"Tucker's parents live in St. Louis, but I think Tucker is taking Wyatt to our grandfather's farm. It's just outside of Hannibal, Missouri," Cole told him.

Sam looked at Cole distrustingly. "What makes you think that?"

"In the letter he says he wants to go back to a time of

innocence and dreams. We used to dream about being Huck Finn and traveling down the Mississippi River on a boat, in the hayloft of our grandfather's barn. I had forgotten about that until I read the letter. I guess Tucker never forgot."

Sam looked at Cole and wondered if he could trust him. His son's life hung in the balance, and there had been times over the last few days when his gut instinct had screamed at him not to trust the other man. Whenever the mistrust reared its ugly head, Cole came through with just enough information to bring him back into the investigation. Sam wondered if he should trust his instincts or if Cole really was innocent and just wanted to bring his cousin in.

Alec pulled him aside and warned, "This could be a trap. This man, Tucker Briggs, is playing a dangerous game with you."

Sam looked his partner straight in the eye. "I know, but he's got my son and I want him back."

"Wyatt was alive tonight, but he may not be when you get to Hannibal," Alec reminded him. "This guy wouldn't think twice about slitting his throat."

Sam pushed Alec away from him and growled, "I can't think about that. I have to believe that Tucker won't hurt him. For reasons only he knows, Tucker Briggs has dragged me into this little game of his, and I have to play it out to the end. He's got the leverage right now, and he's smart enough to know that once that leverage is gone, my incentive to let him live might be gone as well."

"At least you can get there faster by car," Alec pointed out. "It's only about eight hundred miles to Hannibal from here. If he's on the river it could take him a few days."

"If we leave right now we could be there by tomorrow afternoon," Sam suggested, looking at Cole.

Cole nodded. "I could drive a couple of hours, but by then we'll both need to get some rest. Why don't we get some rest now and start off fresh around daybreak?"

Sam realized he and the others were tired. He nodded and told them to follow him back to his house. They could all sleep there, and he and Cole could leave from there in a few hours.

When they pulled up in front of the house Sam shared with his family, the fact that there wasn't anyone there to meet him hit Sam with a terrible blow. Chloe was gone, and their son might never come home. Even Tessa wasn't there anymore. Rage and hatred began filtering into his soul where love had once been, and the rage he felt toward another human being scared him.

As Sam opened the front door and let the others into his world, he looked around the home he'd once had. Everything was the way Chloe had left it just before she'd died. Sam hadn't paid too much attention to the details, but looking at the home Chloe had made for them, he realized that without her and Wyatt this home was just an empty house.

"Is anyone besides me hungry?" Alec asked. When the others all nodded, Sam suggested they order a pizza.

No one could sleep right now anyway. A half hour later, Sam, Rob, Ian, and Alec sat around the living room discussing what they thought would happen next.

"If we leave just before daylight, we should get to the farm around nightfall. We can set up in the hayloft and wait for Tucker. It will take him at least another three or four days to get there," Cole suggested.

"Are you sure he'll travel by river?" Sam asked between bites of pizza. A plan was forming in his mind, and he needed to know. He was only going through the motions of eating. He had no appetite but knew his body needed nourishment.

Cole shrugged. "He's got the houseboat, and he doesn't know that we know that's how he travels. He can hide the houseboat on the river easier than a car on the road."

"I think maybe we should travel by boat," Sam suggested to no one in particular. He wiped his mouth with a napkin and waited for the response.

"Why?" Alec threw his food down on the plate and looked at Sam as if he'd taken leave of his senses.

"Because he might be able to find him on the river," Cole answered for Sam. "It would take at least four, maybe five days to get to Hannibal by boat. He would have that long to look for Tucker and Wyatt."

"What happens if you don't find him on the river?" Ian asked.

"I have to try." Sam couldn't allow himself to think negatively. His whole world depended on getting Wyatt back alive. "If Tucker is out on the river, then that's where I will be. At least I'll be that much closer to Wyatt if I'm there."

"I'm going with you in the morning," Cole said.

"Why?" Sam asked, still not trusting the other man.

"You may find this hard to believe, but all I want is to get your son back and get Tucker the help he needs," Cole told him.

"Your cousin is a killer. He needs to be sitting on death row waiting for the day a needle gets shoved in his arm," Sam said firmly. "And when we catch him, that's where I'll put him—on death row, not in some blasted hospital!"

"You seem awfully confident that you can catch him. That's the second time you said *when*, not *if*," Rob remarked. "How do you plan on doing that?"

"Any way I can." He glared at Cole. "Any objections?"

Cole looked at Sam. "Let's find him first. What happens after that will be up to a court of law."

A few hours later, as dawn broke over the eastern horizon, Sam and Cole were already on the river, preparing to leave. They had woken up the local boat renter and chosen a houseboat. Armed with navigational maps, they plotted their course.

Ian told them before they left that he would contact the police along their route in case they needed assistance. Sam looked at the river ahead of him and couldn't help but think about his son being up there somewhere.

As they stowed groceries for the trip, Alec surprised Sam by handing him his hunting rifle. Sam had often admired the rifle, and Alec had often teased Sam that the only time he would ever let him touch it was when hell froze over.

"Hell might not be freezing over, but you'll need a little extra edge," Alec told him as he gave him the weapon. "Bring the boy back alive, will you?"

"I can't imagine it any other way," Sam told his partner.

"Watch your back," Alec told him. He nodded at Cole and knew he didn't have to explain to Sam what he meant. Alec didn't trust Cole either.

"If you hear anything about Cole, you'll let me know, won't you? I'm not really sure about his part in all this, and I know what he says his motive is, but I don't know him well enough to trust him completely," Sam said. "There's more to this than what he's telling us."

Alec knew him well enough to guess what he was asking him to do. He looked away as he nodded. "I'll check into it for you and let you know what I find."

As Sam boarded the boat, Alec tossed him the mooring lines. Neither said what they were thinking, but they had been partners long enough that words weren't really necessary. That didn't mean Alec didn't say a prayer for what lay ahead. He had a feeling Sam would need all the help he could get.

Chapter Eight

As Sam steered the houseboat north, much of the beauty of the Mississippi River escaped his notice. All he could think about was the fate of his son in the hands of a killer.

He knew that the eight hundred land miles between New Orleans and Hannibal would be considerably more when traveling by river, and that the journey would take longer than a couple of days. He also knew that he had to control the quiet desperation he felt growing inside him. He couldn't afford to make any mistakes. He couldn't let his imagination run loose about what Wyatt was going through either. That would only turn him into a blithering idiot, and he needed to keep focused on the matter at hand.

Cole stood at the front of the boat. While Sam knew what his motive was, he wondered just how far Cole would go to protect his criminal cousin. Sam knew he'd have to keep an eye on the other man.

Cole raised the binoculars to his eyes and watched the river. Tucker regularly traveled by boat and probably knew each turn and every backwater route between here and Hannibal, but he might not know them well enough to chance traveling at night. If Tucker had had to wait until daybreak to leave New Orleans, it was possible that he wasn't that far ahead of them.

"What are you doing?" Sam asked. "He's got at least a four-hour head start."

"Are you sure about that? Maybe he had to wait until first light just like we did," Cole commented. He wasn't going to overlook any possibility.

Sam didn't respond. He didn't feel much like talking anyway. The morning went by quickly, but not quickly enough. They were making good progress, but the houseboat wasn't exactly a speedy form of transport. They could see signs by the water's edge that told them of upcoming towns along the river, and according to the map and their traveling speed Sam figured they would make it to the Arkansas/Mississippi border by nightfall. He couldn't help but wonder where Tucker and Wyatt were right now.

Sam glanced at his watch and found it was almost noon. He shut down the engine and drifted for a while. He glanced over at Cole and asked, "Do you want to eat something?"

Cole nodded, and they went down to the cabin. They each fixed a sandwich and, grabbing a can of soda, returned to the deck. The afternoon sun beat down on them as they ate their lunch. It was Cole who broke the silence by asking, "So, what do I have to do to get you to trust me?"

Sam looked at him briefly before switching his gaze back to the river. "Do you really care if I trust you or not?"

Cole thought for a moment, then nodded his head. "Yeah, I think I do. I know I wasn't as honest with you in the beginning as I should have been, but now we're in this little adventure together. In fact, we are all the other one has." He hesitated and then told Sam, "I think you should know something. I spoke with my boss before we left, and he told me that we had to work together on this. Apparently Ian told him that together we have the best chance of finding Tucker, but alone neither of us has a shot. So yeah, I guess I do care whether you trust me or not." Cole shifted in his chair. "It looks like we have our own reasons for this mission, and neither of us can say it isn't personal."

Sam thought about this statement of fact for a moment and nodded. "Okay, I can see your point. Let me point out something, though. I have the feeling that you're only sharing information on Tucker Briggs on a need-to-know basis. Only when it's absolutely necessary do you come across with just enough information to satisfy us. You never give us any more than we ask, and that makes me think you're still holding back information we need in order to catch him."

Cole nodded. "Okay, fair enough. Ask me anything you want to know, and I'll try to answer." He hesitated, then continued. "But please understand something. This man is someone I shared my childhood with. We went to family gatherings together, we shared our dreams, and we did the same things siblings did. For a while we were closer than brothers. I don't know what turned him into a killer, and I may never find the answer to that question. I would like to see him get the help he needs."

"I think he chose to become a killer. If what you say is true, he had the same advantages you did, the same upbringing, and the same values. What turned him into a killer and you into a cop?" Sam asked. "I think each of us is born with our own sense of worth. Some of us get it beaten out of us, while others nurture it and some-how retain the values and morals needed to get along in this world. You apparently did the latter, while your cousin gave his away to the baser side of life. At some point in his childhood he connected with the wrong side, and it led him straight into evil."

Sam shook his head. "I'm probably not explaining this right. I'm not blaming anybody. I'm sure his parents are very good people, but the choices we make have consequences. Your cousin chose the wrong path, and as long as we are being honest with each other, if he hurts my son in any way, I won't hesitate to kill him. I just want you to know that."

Cole nodded slowly. Sam's insight had helped him understand his cousin a little better. It also lessened the degree of guilt Cole felt. Sam had leveled with him, and he knew Sam would do just what he said he would if the need arose, but Cole would be right there to prevent that from happening.

When Sam started up the boat again, Cole took up his position searching the river. As the afternoon passed, they found no sign of Tucker's boat. They made it to the Arkansas border just as the sun was dipping below the western horizon. They pulled into a small river town called Readland.

Sam docked up the river a little way near a spot called Bert's Place. It looked like a filling station and grocery store on the water's edge. While Cole filled the gas tanks, Sam entered the store. He saw a man sitting behind the counter and a lady stocking shelves. He nodded to both of them and began looking around.

The little store carried just about anything a person could want, from live bait to chicken noodle soup. Before they left New Orleans, Sam had stocked the galley on the boat, so he really didn't need anything from the store. He was just waiting for Cole to fill the gas tank. He approached the old man. "Can a person travel this stretch of river at night?"

The man took the toothpick out of his mouth and shook his head. "Not unless that person knew where the shallows are, and they're shifting all the time. It would probably be best to tie up and wait until daylight."

Sam nodded. He had figured as much, but it didn't hurt to ask. "I'm looking for a friend of mine, Tucker Briggs. Do you know him?"

The man nodded and laughed. "Sure, we know Tucker. He was just here about four hours ago."

"How well do you know him?" Sam asked. His heart rate sped up with the knowledge that they were so close to Tucker and Wyatt.

"Oh, he's been coming by here about three times a year for the last ten years or so, always in the same old houseboat," the man told Sam. "Of course I didn't recognize him at first. He was in a new boat."

Cole finished filling the tanks and came into the store. The man's jaw dropped and the woman stocking the shelves called out Tucker's name. Cole just smiled. "I'm not Tucker, ma'am. I'm his cousin Cole."

The man introduced himself as Bert Carmichael and said the woman was his wife, Letty. Letty looked over at her husband. "Are you sure you're cousins? It's just that you look so much like him, you two could be brothers."

Cole nodded. "Yes, ma'am—our fathers were twin brothers, and our mothers were also twins. Tucker and I used to switch places a lot as kids."

Letty smiled. "I'll bet that was enough to confuse most people." She leaned closer and nodded. "Now I can see a difference between you and Tucker. You're both handsome men, but there's a ruggedness to Tucker that you don't have."

"You're not the first person to notice that," Cole admitted.

"Well, at least Tucker's little boy won't be mistaken for anyone's twin. He must take after his mother though, because he sure doesn't look like his dad." Letty shook her head.

Cole glanced at Sam. Sam was about to say something and Cole wanted him to shut his mouth. "Did Tucker have his son with him?" Cole asked. "I'm surprised by that. The boy's mother has a problem with Tucker being on the river so much."

Bert nodded. "Tucker explained all that. He told us that he felt it was time the boy learned about what was important to him. It seems the boy's been having some problems dealing with the divorce and all the stuff that goes with splitting up a household."

Cole agreed. "Yes, it was a shame Tucker and his wife couldn't have worked things out, but that's life. Everything nowadays is a gamble."

"Well, when you catch up with Tucker, you tell him that Bert and Letty say hi," Bert told them.

Sam stepped up to pay for the gas, and as they left the store, Sam told Cole, "It really is a shame that Tucker's marriage didn't last."

"Well, I couldn't very well tell them the truth, could I?" Cole remarked. "They wouldn't have understood that their friend Tucker was wanted for murder and kidnapping. This way we got the information we needed, and they aren't going to run to their phone and call someone upriver to warn Tucker that we're after him."

Sam nodded. He hadn't thought about that. At least he knew Wyatt was alive and that Tucker was passing him off as his own son. He was still ahead of them, but Sam was confident that Tucker would feel safe enough to slow down when he got farther away from New Orleans, and that's when they would catch up with him. Sam pulled the boat over to the docking area and tied it up for the night. He wasn't about to risk hitting a shallow and having to be towed off while in his pursuit of his son.

By the time the sun hit the halfway point on the second day, Sam and Cole felt they were making progress. They had Arkansas on the left and Mississippi to their right. They were actually seeing more of the river life on the second day than they had the day before. There was still no sign of Tucker, but Sam understood his means of travel a little better.

With the gentle lapping of water on the sides of the boat and the incredible beauty only seen on the river, Sam knew he could get used to this kind of carefree life. The slow, easygoing pace of life on the water was evident in the people. Yesterday they had been in too much of a hurry to see it, but today Sam and Cole saw the river in a different light.

The water was calling to them, seducing them as they plowed through its gentle swells, and the pull of its current was taking them farther and farther from the city sounds of rushing traffic and unbearable noise. Out on the water it was quiet, and you could actually hear the sounds of nature.

Sam was checking his navigational charts when Cole brought him a sandwich and a beer.

"So, how far do you think we'll get by sundown?" Cole asked, as he bit into his sandwich.

"We should get at least to Helena, Mississippi. We'll have to stop around there for gas anyway," Sam told him.

"How much farther ahead of us is he, do you wonder?" Cole finally asked the question on both of their minds.

"I wish I knew," Sam replied as he looked at the huge expanse of river ahead of him. They had been passing swampland and river islands all day. For all they knew, Tucker could be on one of those islands right now. Cole had been searching as far as he could see, but it would have been easy enough to hide a boat if you really wanted to. They had to hope that he was still making his way north to Hannibal.

"What do you think of our chances? Of finding him and Wyatt, I mean," Cole clarified.

Sam thought for a moment, and then nodded. "Actually, I think we made the right decision about traveling by river. We have the element of surprise on our side, and in this sort of game we need every advantage we can get. He doesn't know we followed him by river, and he won't be looking for us until he gets to Hannibal."

Cole nodded.

Sam looked out at the river again and couldn't help but think about Wyatt. He wondered if he was all right or if he was scared. He hoped he was all right. If nothing else, Sam was sure that Wyatt knew he was on his way.

"What do you think will happen once we get to Hannibal?" Cole asked. His intentions of getting his cousin the help he needed were looking more and more impossible, but he needed to hear Sam actually say the words.

Sam took a sip of his beer. "What do you want me to say?" Sam asked after a long pause. "The man is a killer, cousin or not. I'll do everything I can to bring him in alive, but I hope you understand that I can't let him go."

"I didn't expect you would let him go. I was just wondering whether you would shoot him on sight."

Sam shook his head. "I'll bring him in and let the courts decide how to punish him. I'm a cop, and it's part of my job." Sam leaned toward Cole. "But know this, that as a husband and a father I'd like to see him pay, personally, for what he's done to my family."

Cole nodded. "You aren't alone in that regard. The families of the seven other women he's murdered all want justice too." Cole said it in a way that reminded Sam that other people had been hurt by Tucker's actions as well.

Sam looked at the river and didn't say anything as he got the boat under way again. He had forgotten for a moment about Tucker's other activities. All he had been able to think about was his own family. He could feel the sands of time running out. The longer Wyatt was alone with Tucker, the less Sam liked it. Sam looked over at Cole and saw that he'd taken up his position with the binoculars.

The sun was getting low in the sky when they rounded yet another bend in the river. The marker claimed Helena was only a few more miles. Sam checked the gas tank and prayed they would make it that far. River traffic had picked up a bit, and they were seeing more small settlements along the riverbanks.

Sam saw a gas and tackle shop ahead, and as he pulled up to the dock, Cole jumped out and tied off the boat. Cole had donned a fishing hat and a pair of sunglasses and tried not to make contact with anyone as he pumped the fuel.

Earlier that day they had come upon another houseboat, and the owners greeted Cole like a long-lost friend. Again Cole had to pretend to be Tucker and fool the people his cousin knew as friends. It had been decided that, to keep that from happening too much, Cole had to stay belowdecks and avoid contact with people on the river.

As Sam jumped off the boat and ventured inside the tackle shop, something caught Cole's attention. Off to the side of the boat a red baseball cap bobbed in the water. Cole snatched the cap and looked it over and found a name written in black marker: WYATT SEBASTIAN. Cole stood up and looked around. The cap hadn't been in the water long—the fabric wasn't soaked through.

Sam came up behind him. "Did you see something?" he asked.

Cole handed him the hat without taking his eyes off the river.

Sam took an invisible punch to the chest when he saw the hat. For a moment he couldn't breathe as he stared at the red baseball cap he'd bought for his son's Little League practice. Wyatt had been so proud of that hat.

"Do you see anything?" Sam growled as he looked around as well.

"No, but the hat hasn't been in the water for too long.

They must have come through here within the last hour or so," Cole told him.

Sam looked up and down the river as far as he could see. "This is a big place. He could be just about anywhere."

Cole untied the lines holding the boat to the jetty. "We could park somewhere and have a look around."

Sam nodded. "But let's do it right. I don't want Tucker to find us before we find him. Right now he thinks he's safe, and I want him to go right on thinking that. We can't afford any mistakes."

Cole nodded and got on the boat. Sam started the engine and pulled it off the main channel, to a spot where they could see just about every boat in the area.

At that very moment, Tucker Briggs and Wyatt Sebastian were parked for the night just down the river. Tucker had half hidden the boat as a safety precaution, an old habit of his. He had left Wyatt in the soundproof room, also a safety measure. Evening on the river was his time to reflect.

Tonight he was thinking about what he was going to do with the kid he had locked up.

He had called his good buddy Jasper Wiley when he hit the area, and they were supposed to get together later tonight. Tucker had just come up on deck when he got a heads-up from Jasper. Tucker smiled as he watched his buddy climb aboard the boat.

Jasper Wiley was a river rat. He lived and worked on the river. He knew every bend and curve within a hundred miles. He always said the river was like a woman, always changing and never very forgiving. His tall, lean body was tan year-round, and as he climbed aboard Tucker's boat, he let Tucker know he had a bit of gossip to tell. "Hey, good buddy, I hear you got woman trouble." Jasper smiled at Tucker.

Tucker frowned. "I got what?"

Jasper laughed out loud. "I ran into old Bert on the CB today. He said to tell you to take good care of your boy. He also said that your cousin was by his place yesterday. He said he looked so much like you it nearly gave the old man a heart attack."

Tucker's frown turned into a scowl. "He said he ran into my cousin yesterday?"

Jasper nodded. Setting a brown paper bag on the table, he opened it and pulled out a couple of beers. He threw one to Tucker and settled into a deck chair.

Tucker caught the cold brew and began looking around the marina. If Cole was at Bert's place yesterday, he could very well be this far by now. He cursed as he finally caught sight of the boat that Sam and Cole were on. He watched as they continued to look over each and every boat in the area. It was only by luck that they hadn't seen him yet.

Jasper looked at his friend in concern. "What's wrong?"

Tucker stepped back from view. He was busy thinking about how he was going to escape. He wasn't ready for the showdown with Sam and Cole just yet.

"Where's your boat?" Tucker asked Jasper.

"Why? What's wrong with this boat?" Jasper asked in confusion.

"There isn't anything wrong with this boat," Tucker told him. "But I need to get out of here right now, and if I take this boat out on the water, I'm going to be found, and that is something I don't want to happen—at least not yet."

Jasper shook his head. "I don't understand."

Tucker smiled. "My cousin and I are playing a game. I have something he wants to get back." Tucker leaned over the table and pointed to where Cole and Sam were parked. "That's my cousin's boat. If I hang around here, he's going to find me, and I don't want him to—not yet anyway."

Jasper smiled slyly. "Do you need me to run a little interference, maybe get him to follow me for a day or so?"

Tucker shook his head. "No, he'd find you and probably arrest you. Just loan me your boat and wait a day or so and meet me in Hannibal. We'll switch boats then."

Jasper's smile faded. "What would he arrest me for? Is he a cop?"

Tucker grinned. "No, but the guy with him is. My cousin Cole is FBI."

Jasper paled. "FBI? Are you sure you're not in trouble? I don't want any part of that."

Tucker laughed. "My granddad set the whole game thing up. He wanted the two of us boys to compete in a race. The rules were that we both had to leave New Orleans at the same time," Tucker lied. "Whichever of us beat the other to his farm in Hannibal first would get the lion's share of his estate. I thought I was ahead of Cole, but he caught up. Just once I'd like to beat him at something."

Jasper nodded. "I know the feeling. My family thinks my older brother practically walks on water. I have the black boat moored over beyond those trees." Jasper pointed away from Cole and Sam.

Tucker smiled. The game just got a little more interesting. "Do you think you could distract them while I make my getaway?"

Jasper nodded and slipped over the side of the boat. Tucker went below and unlocked the door to the soundproof room. He gathered his things and grabbed Wyatt. Hustling him off the boat and over to Jasper's boat took little effort, and when he looked back to where Cole and Sam's boat was, he saw that Jasper had done what he'd asked. Cole and Sam were looking in the wrong direction.

Tucker started the black boat's engine and carefully maneuvered it out onto the river. He pulled away from the area and moored it downstream about five miles. After checking the area carefully, he set the anchor. Peeking in on Wyatt, he noted the boy was still tied up. He knew the boy was too afraid of him to try anything, so Tucker felt safe in leaving him alone for a while. He wanted to go back and see what Cole and Sam were up to. They caught him off guard today, and Tucker didn't like being caught off guard.

Using the dinghy, he made his way back to Helena and began looking around the marina. When he spotted their boat, he sat in the dinghy and watched them for a while. They seemed to be settling in for the night.

Tucker knew he should be as far away from them as possible, but he also knew the harbor was full of his friends and they would protect him if the need arose. All the people on the river protected one another from outsiders. This was their way of life, and most of them wouldn't have it any other way. He was surprised that Cole and Sam had come on the river after him. He knew it had been Cole's idea. His plan had almost worked.

Cole shifted in his chair on the deck of the house-boat. He had an uneasy feeling. Something was niggling the hairs on the back of his neck, and he knew he should be a little more alert. He looked out on the river, and at first he didn't notice the little dinghy parked not too far away from him. Then something splashed in the water and Cole looked a little harder.

Out in the middle of the channel sat his cousin Tucker. Cole had to be sure, so he got up and reached for the binoculars sitting on the console. Raising them to his eyes, he focused on the dinghy. Catching his breath in a hiss, he watched as Tucker gave him a royal salute.

Cole lowered the binoculars and handed them to Sam. "Look out toward the middle of the river and tell me that you see him too."

Sam frowned and brought the binoculars to his eyes. "He's there. I don't believe it. The creep is just sitting there."

"So much for the element of surprise," Cole said.

"Why is he just sitting there?" Sam asked, not taking his eyes off the dinghy or the man inside it.

"I think he's telling us that our being here isn't going to bother him too much. He knows we can't go after him in the dark. For now he has the advantage."

"Where is my gun?" Sam muttered.

"It wouldn't do you much good anyway," Cole said.

Sam dropped the binoculars and glared at Cole. "Why not?" said.

"Because even if you hit him, you'd lose the only chance you have of finding your son—in case you haven't noticed, the boy isn't with him," Cole pointed out.

Sam grumbled and brought the binoculars back to his eyes and watched Tucker for a minute or two. "What I'd like to know is how he knew we were here."

"That doesn't matter anymore. He knows, and now it's a race to see who will win," Cole stated.

They both heard the dinghy's motor start up, and within minutes Tucker was gone. Sam was more than disappointed. He had been within reaching distance, and there was nothing he could do. Sam was getting more than tired of playing Tucker's game.

Chapter Nine

Around midnight Sam was startled awake by the ring of his cell phone. He had been trying unsuccessfully to get some kind of rest for his weary body. He grabbed the phone and when he whispered hello, he heard Wyatt's voice.

"Dad, are you there?" Wyatt's voice was trembling and unsure, but it was the sweetest thing Sam had heard in days.

"Wyatt, thank God! Are you okay?" Sam spoke softly so as not to scare away the voice on the phone. He sat up on the edge of the bed. Tears of joy and relief burned his eyes.

"Yeah, I'm okay. Where are you?" Wyatt asked.

There was silence on the phone for a moment, and then another voice came on the line. "Yeah, Dad, where are you?"

Sam's relief hardened into rage at the sound of the other voice. "I'm right behind you, jerk."

Tucker Briggs laughed. "That's what you think." The call was abruptly cut off.

Sam reached over and snapped on the light on the bedside table. Cole groaned from the bed next to his as the light came on. Propping himself up on one elbow, he looked at Sam. "What's going on?"

"Your cousin just called."

Cole sat up in bed. "How did he get your number?"

"He had Wyatt dial it."

Sam stood and pulled on his pants. Grabbing his phone, he left the room. Cole joined him a few minutes later.

Cole sat down quietly in one of the deck chairs and waited for Sam to speak. "What is he up to now?" Sam asked.

Cole reached inside his pocket and pulled out a cigarette. He usually didn't smoke, but the stress of the last few days had gotten to him. He waited until the cigarette was lit before he answered. "Tucker is playing mind games with you."

"What?" Sam whirled around and stared at Cole. "How do you know that?"

Cole nodded. "Because that's what Tucker does. He's very good at them too. As a kid he could manipulate people into doing anything he wanted. He knew just which buttons to push. He knows that Wyatt is your button."

"Wyatt is my son, not a button," Sam growled.

Cole nodded. "But to get to you, he'll give you just a taste of your son, and then he'll snatch him back. Tonight was that taste. Tucker will call you back, but he won't let you talk to Wyatt again, not until it suits his purpose."

Sam was beginning to understand, and he didn't like it. "I wonder what he meant."

"Meant by what?" Cole asked as he flicked the cigarette over the side of the boat.

"When I told Wyatt that I was right behind him, Tucker said that's what *I* thought," Sam told Cole.

Cole swore.

Sam turned to look at him.

Cole had a frown on his face. "That means he got ahead of us in the last few hours. After he left in the dinghy, he must have pulled out."

Sam glanced at his watch. It was only two A.M. They had several hours until daylight. He looked north. At the moment the river looked serene, its gentle lapping hiding a host of secrets. Tucker knew those secrets, and Sam didn't. For the moment, Tucker had the advantage, but if he thought for a second that Sam was giving up, he didn't know Sam very well.

"Do you want to try and follow him?" Cole asked.

Sam shook his head. "He knows this river too well. We have to wait for daylight, and he knows it."

Cole stood up. "I'm sorry. I wish there was something I could do."

"Go get some rest. Tomorrow is going to be a long day. One of us needs to be alert," Sam told him.

Cole looked at Sam. "You need to rest too."

Sam nodded. "I know, but I just can't sleep right now. I'll stay up here for a while."

Once he was alone, Sam had time to think. He sat down in the chair Cole had vacated and stared out at the river. The serenity surrounding him calmed his raging soul but did little to quiet his thoughts.

About an hour later his phone rang again. By that time Sam had calmed down enough to regain his composure, and he knew what was coming. He answered the call.

Tucker's voice came over the line. "Isn't the river peaceful tonight?"

"You know, I think I know why you travel this way. It is peaceful. Not like being stuck in the middle of the city, with all the noise and constant interruptions," Sam told him.

"Yeah, out on the river you can hear yourself think." He hesitated, and then said, "You surprised me."

"How?" Sam asked.

"You followed me on the river. I wasn't expecting that."

"You took my son. Did you really think I wouldn't come after you to get him back?" Sam asked quietly.

Tucker chuckled. "I underestimated you. Don't worry, I won't do that again."

"Did you call just to tell me how quiet it is on the river, or did you have something else to say?" Sam asked.

"Aren't you interested in how your boy is doing?"

Sam's hand tightened around the phone, but that was the only outward sign of tension. "I know he's still alive, and you'd better keep him that way."

"Why should I?" Tucker wanted to know.

"Because if anything happens to him, I will hunt you down and take great pleasure in ending your miserable life."

Sam spoke with such conviction that even Tucker was taken aback by his tone. After a moment of silence, Tucker told him, "You have to catch me first." Then the line went dead.

Sam smiled to himself. He'd given Tucker something to think about. The other man had to wonder just how far Sam would go, and that might be enough to keep him off balance and even things up again.

Dawn was just breaking when Cole woke up to the engine humming underneath him. Glancing at the window, he saw the early-morning light filtering through and knew that Sam couldn't wait any longer. He joined Sam up on deck a few minutes later.

Sam looked disheveled. Cole doubted he'd gotten any sleep. He desperately needed a shave and hadn't combed his hair. Cole didn't say a word, but instead turned around and went below. He needed to make some coffee. A few minutes later, Sam killed the motor and yelled. Cole came running back on deck.

Cole looked at Sam and then followed his line of sight. There, half hidden by trees, was the boat on which Tucker had left New Orleans.

Sam restarted the boat and brought it in closer to Tucker's boat. Tucker's boat looked deserted, but it was early, so not that many people were up and about yet.

Cole disappeared below, and when he reappeared he had Sam's gun in one hand and his own in the other. They both boarded Tucker's boat.

Cole took one side, and Sam took the other, and together they searched the deck. As they made their way below, everything was quiet. When they reached the sleeping quarters, the door was closed. Sam reached out a hand and turned the knob. He nodded at Cole and shoved the door open. Both men rushed into the room with their guns ready.

Looking around, they found only a strange man passed out on the big double bed. An empty bottle of liquor lay beside his unconscious body. Empty beer cans littered the cabin floor.

Sam shoved the gun into the waistband of his pants and reached down and grabbed the unconscious man. Shaking him awake, he began asking questions.

Jasper groaned and opened one eye. He found Sam scowling at him. "Who are you, and where is the owner of this boat?" Sam shook him again. "Where is Tucker Briggs?"

"Who?" Jasper asked, still not thinking straight. He swallowed hard.

Sam leaned closer to the man. "I asked you who you are and where Tucker Briggs is, and you'd better tell me right now. Where is he?"

Jasper swallowed hard again. "My name is Jasper Wiley and I don't know where Tucker is. He left last night."

Cole asked, "How do you know Tucker?"

Jasper didn't take his eyes off Sam. "I've known Tucker for about ten years," Jasper said. "We go fishing together when he's in the area."

"How did he leave?" Sam asked.

"He borrowed my boat." Jasper wasn't going to tell him anything, but one look at Sam's face made him change his mind. Jasper wasn't sure what Tucker had done to Sam, and he wasn't sure he wanted to know. Jasper had to wonder just what he'd gotten himself into.

"What kind of boat did he borrow?" Sam demanded.

Three hours later they were almost to the Missouri border. Cole was scanning the river with the binoculars while Sam steered. They knew now they were looking for a black houseboat called *Jasper's Folly*, and they weren't wasting any time getting to their destination. It would be sometime tomorrow before they would reach Hannibal, but Sam was determined to get as far as he could today.

As they passed another river island, Sam had a terrible thought. Would Tucker Briggs be crazy enough to leave a six-year-old boy out alone on one of the islands between here and Hannibal? Sam killed the boat's engine. Cole turned around and looked at him.

"You don't think your cousin would leave Wyatt on one of these islands, do you?" he asked Cole. "As sort of a bargaining chip, I mean? In case we run into him again, that is."

Cole frowned and hesitated. He looked at the island

they had just passed and then he looked north at another. The thought alone was horrendous, but was Tucker willing to go that far? *Hell,* Cole thought, *he's done worse.* "I don't know. I simply don't know if he would do that or not. I would hope not, but he's done worse things, I guess."

"That's why I asked," Sam said.

"If we take the time to check, he'll probably beat us to Hannibal. He's got a lead on us now. It won't slow us up too much to just have a quick look. At least then we would know for sure," Cole told Sam.

Sam steered the boat closer to the next island they came to. Both he and Cole looked over the island as well as they could without docking the boat. There didn't seem to be anyone on the island. They moved upriver and stopped at the next island. Traveling this way was a lot slower, but at least they knew that Wyatt wasn't on any of them.

By mid-afternoon Sam and Cole were exhausted, sunburned, and starving. Sam called it a day. He wanted to push on, but his body was near collapse.

Sam stopped the boat's engine, and without a word to Cole, he disappeared belowdecks. Cole picked up Sam's cell phone and placed a call. A few minutes later he started the engine, and slowly took the boat north.

Hours later, the sun was down and the heat of the day was cooling from the river. It was a clear night, and the full moon lending its brilliance to the night sky was reflected in the calm river. Sam rejoined Cole on deck.

"Where are we?" Sam asked finally, not recognizing anything around them.

"We're just south of a little town in Tennessee called Golddust," Cole told him as he sat on a deck chair sipping a beer. The empty plate beside him told Sam that Cole had at least eaten something.

He disappeared belowdecks and reappeared with a sandwich and a beer. He sat next to Cole and began to eat. "So, how far did we come today?" he asked Cole between bites.

Cole looked out onto the river. "Not as far as I would have liked. I've been checking each island as we passed it, but I haven't seen anything."

Sam nodded. "It's possible that we've been wasting our time, but you have to understand, I had to be sure."

Cole nodded. "I understand completely. If Wyatt was my son, I would have expected no less from you. I can't fault you for being a good parent." He took another sip of his beer, and then told Sam, "I called my uncle this afternoon."

Sam was bringing the bottle up to his mouth for a drink and hesitated. Then he put the bottle to his lips and took a swallow. He set it back on the table and grabbed his sandwich. "And what did your uncle have to say?"

"They haven't seen or heard from Tucker in ten years. They had no idea what he's been doing either. Ethan couldn't believe what I had to say," Cole told him.

"Did you tell them what Tucker has been up to?" Sam asked.

Cole shook his head. "I couldn't. Ethan and Joyce

wouldn't understand. Hell, there are times when I think all this is nothing more than a nightmare myself."

"I would still like to know why he picked my family to destroy," Sam said.

"I guess we'll just have to wait and ask him when we catch up to him," Cole replied.

"Do you still think he's going to Hannibal?" Sam had to ask.

Cole nodded. There was something else he had to tell Sam. "Ethan told me something I didn't know before today. He told me that Tucker has made several trips up to Hannibal in the last few years. He and my dad never know when he's coming, but they always know when he's been there."

"How do they know that?"

Cole shrugged. "He said it was a lot of little things. Tucker never leaves a note or anything, but he said some of the furniture gets moved around sometimes, or they've noticed pictures are missing and later returned. He said one time Tucker's mom put out a quilt on his bed that she had made for him, and the next time they checked the house, the quilt was gone."

"Why does he go there?" Sam asked.

"I've been thinking about all the people that claim to know me as Tucker, and all the different names he's gone by. Paul Moran and Nick Granger are only the ones we know about. When we were teenagers, just before Tucker left, something happened. At the time I thought he was just playing some sort of game. He had me go with him to another city, where he changed his clothes and literally became another person. We were fifteen years old at the time, and he walked into a place of business and began pitching an idea to the manager. The manager called him Tom Reed. As Tom Reed, he made more money in one afternoon than I do in a year's time. His performance was outstanding, and I remember being in awe of him. What if that's what he was doing when you caught him on film? I mean, if you photographed him while he was pretending to be someone else, that might put a serious dent in his bank account. I think we have to dig a little deeper into your theory and find out exactly what he was doing in the park that day. You think he was taking his next victim, but what if it was something else?" Cole suggested.

"Like what?" Sam asked. He frowned. Cole wasn't making any sense.

Cole shrugged. "If he was scamming someone using a false name, he wouldn't want that known. His cover has never been blown before, and he takes great pride in that. But if the wrong person started asking questions, his whole scheme could fall apart."

"Are you suggesting that you think he goes back to Hannibal for money?" Sam asked.

Cole nodded. "I think he would have to find a place that only he knows about, somewhere he figures is safe. He knows that very few people go to the farm anymore. He could find a place that he knows won't be discovered and leave things there—not just money but anything he uses from time to time, like maybe all the aliases he uses, for instance. I mean, he can't exactly put his money in a bank. He wouldn't want to leave a paper trail. Something like that could be discovered by anybody. He's got to have someplace to hide all that stuff. It's not like he can leave it out in the open, and he wouldn't leave it on his boat."

"Is this something you know for a fact, or is it just speculation?" Sam asked.

Cole shrugged. "When I first discovered the killer might be Tucker, I dug into his background but nothing came up. I couldn't find anything from the time he was fifteen and left home. He has no bank account or credit card under his own name anywhere."

Sam thought for a moment. "I think we need to find out more about his trips to Hannibal. Did your uncle say how often he's been there?"

Cole shook his head. "He didn't say."

"How do they know he's been there?" Sam repeated his earlier question.

Cole looked out at the river for a moment and then back at Sam. "You have to understand something. They have no clue what Tucker has been doing all these years. All they know is that he is their son, and good or bad, he is their flesh and blood. It's going to be hard for them to understand what's happened to him."

"That doesn't answer my question." Sam paused and then said, "I think we need to talk to your uncle again and find out for ourselves." Sam's thoughts turned to his young son. He didn't know if he would understand it either, if something like this had happened to him. He wished he could hear his voice again.

As if on cue, his phone rang. Sam looked at Cole and then down at his phone. He quickly grabbed it and said, "Hello."

"I have to say that I'm disappointed in how little distance you covered today. How do you expect to catch me if you can't keep up with me?" Tucker asked.

"Where are you, you creep?" Sam made a low sound in his throat.

"That would be telling, wouldn't it? I hope you don't expect me to do your job for you too?" Tucker taunted Sam. Sam was rattled, but he knew that Tucker was using his feelings to control him.

Sam took a deep breath and got his emotions under control. "Did you call just to chat, or was there something you wanted to tell us?"

"I got bored waiting for you guys to catch up, so I thought I would call and complain," Tucker told him.

"If you're that bored, come on over. I can guarantee that you won't be anymore," Sam promised, and then hesitated. "Let me ask you something."

It was Tucker's turn to pause. "Okay, go ahead and ask. Of course, you may not like the answer, but you can always ask."

"Why me and my family?"

"Ahh, that's the question that has plagued man for centuries. Why me?" Tucker paused. "I would have to say it's because I admire your technique."

"What? What are you talking about?" Sam asked, confused.

"The first time I saw you, I was impressed by the way

you handled a tough situation. You had compassion for the little guy, yet you slapped down the big bad wolf at the same time. You were awesome."

"What are you talking about?"

"I doubt you would remember this, but we met once, a long time ago," Tucker told him.

"I don't think I would have forgotten that," Sam said.

"Oh, but we did. You were investigating a murder case. Robert Cale was murdered by his wife Rebecca. Do you remember the case?"

Sam thought back. He remembered the Cale case, but he didn't remember ever meeting Tucker Briggs. "I remember the case."

"That was the case that brought you into my world. I followed that case in the papers for weeks. You were the only cop who gave a damn, and you didn't quit until the case was solved and the guilty people were in jail."

"What does any of that have to do with why you chose me to play your little game?" Sam asked again. "I still don't remember meeting you."

"We ran into each other one day when you were coming out of the station house." Tucker chuckled. "That was the day your wallet went missing, in fact."

Sam thought for a moment. He did remember misplacing his wallet, but he had found it later, on the floor of his car. He'd thought he'd dropped it there. "How did you know I lost my wallet?"

Sam heard Tucker laugh. "Because you didn't lose it—I swiped it," Tucker boasted.

"Why did you do that?" Sam asked.

"I wanted to know everything I could about you—your family, your interests, your hangouts," Tucker told him.

"Why?" Sam repeated, trying to remember what had been in his wallet.

"I have been looking for just the right person for a long time now, and I chose you," Tucker said simply.

"The right person for what?" Sam asked.

"All my life, there's been a part of me that doesn't fit anywhere. My family didn't see it, my friends didn't see it, and for a long time even I didn't see it. Then one day that part of me came out, and I realized that the something I was always searching for was death itself. The remorse I was supposed to feel when someone close to me died wasn't there. Instead, a sense of total freedom filled my soul. I began experimenting, and I have to be honest with you. The rush I got when I killed something or someone was incredible. The power I felt was amazing. I can't even describe it." Tucker paused for a moment. "I can't seem to stop. I've tried to, but I can't.

"The police haven't been able to stop me either. Not even my cousin Cole has been able to catch me. I chose you because I think you might be the only person who could ever come close to stopping me."

"The items in my wallet told you that?" Sam inquired. "You could have just dropped me a line and asked me to catch you. With your history, I would have tried to find you."

Tucker laughed. "I have everything to lose if you catch me. Let's just say I wanted to even the playing field. I wanted—no, that isn't quite right—I *needed* you to have a personal motive to stay and play the game with me."

"So you killed my wife and kidnapped my son just to make me come after you?" Sam hissed. He was close to losing control again, and he had a feeling that Tucker knew it.

"Doesn't the hatred in your soul keep you coming after me? Doesn't your rage give you the energy to want to find me?"

Sam didn't say anything. Everything Tucker had just said was true. The rage he felt for the man responsible for Chloe's death *was* keeping him going—that and the fact that this evil man had his son.

Chapter Ten

So if I catch you, are you going to come peacefully, or is that a dumb question?" Sam asked.

"I haven't made up my mind yet. We'll have to wait and see if and when that time comes," Tucker told him. "But you have to catch me first, and you aren't even close to doing that, so I guess I won't have to worry for a while."

When Sam didn't respond, Tucker sprinkled a little salt in the wound. "You know, Sam, you have an amazing family. Your wife—now, what was her name?—oh yes, Chloe. Well, let me tell you something—she was a hot little number. If she was my wife, I would have been home every night with bells on."

"Shut up, you little worm," Sam growled at him. "You aren't fit to speak her name."

"Now, is that any way for a father to speak? What if Wyatt had been listening? Oh yeah, I forgot—Wyatt is with me." He laughed, and the sound grated on Sam's nerves.

Sam slammed his phone down on the table. He vowed then and there before this was over he was going to kill that man, with his bare hands if necessary. One way or another, Tucker Briggs was going to die.

Cole knew enough not to ask any questions or offer any comments. He recognized the rage in Sam's eyes and knew that his cousin had put it there. He got up and started the boat. Traveling by moonlight was dangerous, but he had to do something.

They made slow progress through the night. They wasted little time in Golddust, stopping only for gas.

They must have had a guardian angel watching over them that night, because they made good progress and didn't run into anything. At dawn's first light, they were almost to St. Louis.

"So, how far are we from Hannibal?" Sam finally asked.

Cole shrugged. "We have around a hundred and seventy miles or so to go yet."

Sam nodded and fell silent. Finally, he asked Cole, "Is there a reason your cousin has a death wish?"

Cole looked shocked. "What?" He hadn't thought of that possibility.

"I've been thinking about our conversation last night. He told me that he's been looking for just the right person for his little game for a long time now, and I was wondering if there was a reason why."

Cole shook his head. "If there is, then my family and I don't know about it."

Sam nodded. "I was just wondering. He's done enough to warrant a spot on death row, but I won't help him end his life in a police-assisted suicide."

Cole didn't say anything.

Tucker was playing a dangerous game with the wrong person. Sam had made his position very clear. Tucker wouldn't escape justice. When this was all over, he'd either be in jail or dead.

It was late afternoon before they got to Hannibal. They were able to bypass St. Louis, and now as evening approached they neared the dock by Cole's grandfather's farm. They hadn't heard or seen anything of Tucker, and they were a little worried that he'd been there and left already.

Cole pulled the boat into a little cove not too far from the dock, yet where it could remain hidden from sight. As they backtracked to the farm, Sam hid in the tall grass and looked over the river entrance.

Cole waited for him on the path to the barn. When Sam joined him a few minutes later, Cole asked, "Any sign of the boat?"

Sam shook his head. "No, and that worries me. He seemed in an all-fired hurry last night. I can't imagine he would waste a whole day."

Cole looked up toward the barn. "Maybe we should check the barn. If he's been here and gone, there should be some sign in the barn."

Sam nodded, and silently they made their way to

the barn. He readied his gun as Cole pulled open the door. The heavy screech of the old iron hinges echoed in the quietness of the farm. Sam cringed and frowned at Cole.

Cole just shrugged.

The barn was dark inside and smelled of moldy hay and dust. Nobody, except for mice, rats, and the occasional possum, had been inside for years. Cole had previously warned Sam that the utilities had been shut off since his grandfather died, so Sam was prepared when Cole grabbed the flashlight he'd brought from the boat and turned it on. The light barely pierced the darkness, and the fading sunlight would be gone soon.

Sam looked around as much as he could and was satisfied that there was no one in the barn. They couldn't do much in the dark, and he knew that if Tucker was coming it would be in the daylight hours.

Sam turned and motioned for Cole to leave the barn. Outside, he holstered his weapon and asked, "Is there somewhere close by we could stay? I don't want to be far away if Tucker decides to come by here around dawn."

Cole nodded. "Sure, we could stay up at the house. I think my family keeps it clean and stocked with groceries for when they come down. Ethan mentioned that they had all just been here a few weeks ago."

Sam turned to look at the river. The path from the barn to the riverbank was clear. He could see the expanding volume of the water from where he stood. He looked back at the barn. On the second-story loft area he could see a double door that faced the river. From that location, Sam bet he would be able to see quite a bit more of the river. "What exactly did your grandfather raise on this farm?" Sam asked.

"Mostly Cain, my grandmother used to say," Cole told him. "Actually, this farm has quite a history. Back before the Civil War, this farm was used to smuggle goods to the North. During the war, this was one of the underground slave stops. The caves near the water's edge made it a perfect place to hide things."

Sam perked up at this bit of trivia. "Do you know where these caves are?"

Cole nodded. "Sure, Tucker and I used to play in them when we were kids." It was then that the significance of what he had just said seemed to hit Cole. He looked at Sam. "If he needed a safe place to hole up or hide something, he'd use the caves."

Sam grinned. "Let's go to the caves before we go up to the house. We just might find something."

Cole led the way. The overgrown brush made the trip hazardous, but when they reached the entrance, Cole noticed that someone had been keeping it up. There were no footprints in the sand, so they knew Tucker hadn't been there in a while. The entrance was through two boulders and it was a tight squeeze for a grown man, but they made it through.

Just inside the cave they found supplies, candles,

matches, and a gas lantern. Lighting the lantern, they ventured deeper into the cave. When they came to a side cave they looked around it before moving on. The cave seemed to branch off at one point. They followed the left branch, but didn't find anything worthwhile, so they retraced their steps and went the other way. There they came to a wooden door of sorts. Moving the door that had long ago rusted off its hinges, they found what they were looking for.

It was another room, but this one had modern amenities. There was a cot and a battery-powered lamp. Cole switched on the lamp and it illuminated the whole room.

Tucker had everything he needed to stay hidden for days. He had a suitcase, a five-gallon barrel of fresh water, and a few supplies.

Sam walked over to the suitcase and flipped open the top. The inside was filled with papers, some jewelry, and a lot of money. Sam didn't touch the money, but he was interested in the papers. He sat on the cot and began looking through them.

He found Paul Moran's driver's license, as well as a bank card and a stained receipt for the houseboat. The stain looked like blood, but Sam didn't want to hazard a guess at whose.

He also found two other driver's licenses bearing the names of Tom Danvers and Michael Kennedy, and a press ID bearing Michael Kennedy's name.

"Well, at least we know where he goes underground. He could stay here for days," Cole remarked.

"How often does your family come here?" Sam asked.

Cole tried to remember but couldn't. "They come down about six times a year just to make sure that no one has broken into the house. Mom and Aunt Joyce can't bear to part with the house, so it hasn't been sold yet."

Sam motioned around the cave. "I don't suppose you can get to the house from this cave, can you?"

Cole grinned. "Actually, you can, if no one has moved the piano. Come on, I'll show you."

Cole picked up the lantern and led the way. They took the other tunnel and walked deeper into the cave. They came to a stop at the very edge of the cave, and when Cole raised the lantern, Sam saw a wooden ladder leading upward.

Grabbing the ladder, Sam began to climb. He came to the top of the ladder only to find a wooden door. He pushed the door open and found himself inside the house.

"Watch yourself—there's a piano just to your left," Cole called out. Sam grabbed the flashlight and lit the room with it. It was the sitting room, as far as he could tell. He moved away from the door and waited for Cole to climb the ladder.

Cole brought the lantern with him, and soon the house was bathed in light. Sam looked around the room and ventured down the hall. When he returned, Cole shrugged. "I don't know if he's been here or not."

Sam was putting away his weapon when he heard a noise upstairs. He motioned for Cole to douse the light and found his way to the stairway in the dark. As he was about to take the first step up, Cole whispered from behind, "Watch the fifth step—it squeaks."

Sam nodded and carefully made his way upstairs. He stepped over the fifth stair, and when he reached the top he saw a faint light under the door of the bedroom at the end of the hall. Carefully and quietly, he made his way to the bedroom door. Reaching for the doorknob, he turned it and pushed it open.

Tucker Briggs was sitting on the bed. Sam had caught him unaware and unarmed. Tucker just grinned and held up his hands.

"Don't you move an inch, or I will blow you to Kingdom Come." Sam spoke quietly, his rage barely in check.

"If you kill me, you'll never find your kid," Tucker told him.

"Where is he?" Sam asked, pointing his gun at Tucker.

"That's for me to know and you to wonder," Tucker said as he linked his hands behind his head and leaned back against the headboard.

"I *will* kill you," Sam assured him.

"Then I will take your son's whereabouts to the grave with me."

Sam's fingers tightened around the trigger of the gun, and then without warning his head exploded with pain as something hit him from behind. He slumped to the floor.

Tucker grinned and looked beyond Sam. "Cousin, what have you done?"

* * *

Cole looked over at the man on the bed. "Where's the boy?"

Tucker leaned back and smiled. "I don't think I'll tell you that, not yet anyway." He looked at Sam, then back at his cousin. "You know he's going to hate you when he wakes up, don't you?"

"I think you've goaded him as far as you can. He wants his kid back and you dead. I just saved your miserable life," Cole told his cousin.

Tucker's smile grew as he got up off the bed. "Nah, he wasn't going to shoot. I still have something he wants. As long as I have the kid, he won't kill me."

Cole shook his head. Tucker wasn't facing the stark reality of his situation. He watched as his cousin gathered his things and prepared to exit. "Where do you think you're going?" Cole asked.

"I still have things to do. You might consider leaving too, before he comes to. He might just kill you for helping me escape," Tucker told Cole.

"You aren't going anywhere. Sit down." Cole motioned toward the bed. "I didn't knock Sam out to help you escape. I knocked him out because he was going to shoot you."

Tucker's demeanor changed. His smile faded, and his eyes glazed over, his expression cold. This was the killer side of Tucker.

Tucker came toward Cole. He didn't have to reach for the knife on his belt. He just had to walk toward him. "Don't make me kill you, Cousin. I'm going to walk out of here, and the next time we meet, you and I will have issues to settle. Right now I have some other unfinished business to attend to. As long as I'm in the area I might have to go see what's left of my family. Won't they be surprised? I mean, it's been what . . . ten years since I've seen any of them? We'll have so much to catch up on."

Cole knew that if he wanted to, Tucker would kill him. He didn't move, and he didn't try to stop Tucker either. He just let him walk past. When he was gone, Cole took a deep breath.

He sat down on the bed and looked at Sam. What could Cole say to him? How could he justify what he'd done to a man who only wanted his son back? Would Cole get a chance to explain the knock-out blow before Sam killed him?

And what had Tucker meant by his statement about seeing the rest of his family? Ethan had told Cole that they hadn't seen Tucker since he left all those years ago. It could only mean one thing.

Sam groaned as he regained consciousness. His head hurt and when he opened his eyes he saw that Tucker was gone. Sam sat up and held his head for a minute. When the throbbing became tolerable, he blinked his eyes and looked around the room again. The only one he saw was Cole. Had he let Tucker go? They had been after him for almost a week. Sam thought he knew Cole; he had actually begun to trust him.

Sam felt around for his gun. He found it underneath his leg. Picking it up, he cocked the weapon. Then he stood up groggily and took a few steps toward Cole. Pointing the barrel at him, Sam said, "Give me a reason I shouldn't pull this trigger. Make it a good one, because my head is killing me and the noise won't make it any better."

Cole swallowed hard. He wasn't sure he liked this side of Sam. "You were letting him goad you into shooting him. If you had, we would never have found Wyatt."

"What makes you think for a moment that we'll find him now?" Sam asked.

"Because I think I know where Tucker is going," Cole told him.

"And where would that be?" Sam asked.

"St. Louis."

"Why would Tucker go all the way back to St. Louis?"

"I think he's going to kill his entire family," Cole whispered. He couldn't believe it himself, but it was the only thing that made any sense.

Sam frowned. The throbbing in his head worsened, and he had to sit down and hold the top of his head for a moment. When the pain subsided, he looked at Cole. "What did you say?"

"Tucker said he had some unfinished business to attend to, and then he said he was going to see what was left of his family. I think he's going to murder them all."

"Why? Why would you think that?" Sam asked.

Cole struggled to put it into words so that someone else would understand. "Throughout our childhood, people would mistake us for brothers or twins. It was annoying. We were two separate people, yet to the rest of the world we looked identical. Those who knew us considered us opposites—one was good while the other was evil. Every time Tucker got into trouble, Joyce or Ethan would say to him, 'Why can't you be more like Cole?' They were always comparing us to each other, and Tucker always got the short end. It wasn't that he was bad, not all the time. They were, in their own way, too focused on the twin thing. Twins never *act* identically. They are often very different people, two totally separate personalities. They're just two people who look alike. I don't think his parents ever realized just what they were doing to him."

"That doesn't explain why you think he's going to St. Louis," Sam said.

"Tucker wanted to be appreciated for himself. He didn't want to be compared to someone else. They did that every chance they got, until his own identity was washed away. Remember how Jerry Springs thought I was Nick Granger? Tucker became Nick because Nick had something he wanted. It was the same with Paul and the others. Tucker killed them and absorbed their place because he needed a new identity. Joyce and Ethan took his away years ago, and now he wants it back. I think he feels he has to kill them in order to get it."

"You know your cousin a lot better than I do, so I'll take your word for it," Sam told him. He placed the cold steel of his gun against his aching forehead. "Just don't ever try to knock me out again, not even to make a point. Next time I won't give you a chance to explain why you did. I'll just shoot you."

Cole nodded.

Sam stood up and holstered his weapon. Looking at Cole, he asked, "Well, are you coming or are you going to sit there all night? We have to go back to St. Louis."

By the time they got to the boat, there was very little daylight left. If they started out now, it would be dark by the time they got to St. Louis. "Can you drive this thing at night?" Sam asked Cole.

Cole nodded. "I think so. I did last night."

Sam nodded and cast off the tether lines as Cole started the engine. Neither of them spoke much on the journey south. Sam kept the lookout, peering through the ever-darkening skies for Jasper's black boat.

When they reached the port of St. Louis, they wasted very little time at the docks. They hailed a cab and made their way to the address Cole gave the cab driver. So as not to alarm anyone, they chose to get out of the cab at the corner of the block where Ethan and Joyce lived.

As Sam stepped out of the cab, he took a minute to look over the neighborhood. It was late and there were no outward signs of alarm. He wasn't sure if that was good or bad. He paid for the cab and, as it drove away, both men began walking down the block, looking for any sign of Tucker.

Sam and Cole were almost to their target when they reached for their weapons. Holding them at their sides, they approached the house. The lights were on but there was no immediate sign of trouble inside. Cole was reaching for the doorbell when he noticed the door was ajar.

He looked at Sam and motioned toward the door. Sam nodded and raised his gun. Cole did the same. Sam then raised his leg and nudged the door wide open.

Making their way through the foyer to the living room, they began to see signs of a struggle. The television was on with the volume turned up. A table had been overturned and a lamp smashed. But the real conflict appeared to have taken place in the kitchen. As they made their way through they found food and broken dishes strewn across the table and the floor, and when Sam looked more closely he found blood.

Cole left the kitchen and searched the rest of the house. When he returned, he shook his head. "There's no one here."

Sam nodded at the mess. "Well, we know he was here. Where would he take them?"

"The only place I can think of is my grandfather's farm," Cole told him.

"The farm we just left?" Sam groaned.

Cole nodded.

"You're kidding me. Why would he take them back there?" Sam asked.

"Because that's where he arranged the first accident that almost killed them," a voice from the doorway told them.

Cole and Sam spun around in surprise and confronted an older version of Cole.

"Dad?" Cole called out in surprise. "What do you mean 'the first accident'?"

Chapter Eleven

As Roger Davidson came into the kitchen, he was followed by Cole's mother, Emily. Cole was glad to see them both alive and unhurt.

"What did you mean, he arranged an accident? When was this?" Cole asked his parents.

Roger looked at Emily, and then they both looked at Cole and Sam. "It happened so long ago I had almost forgotten about it," Emily began. "At the time we didn't realize just what happened, but when Ethan called us, suddenly it all made sense."

"Excuse me," Sam interrupted. "You said Ethan called you? When did he do that?"

Emily looked at Sam. "After he talked to Cole the other day, he called us to let us know what was going on. At first we thought you were wrong about Tucker, and then we began remembering little things that happened when the two of you were growing up. When you two boys were about seven, Joyce and Ethan were going to have another baby. They were so happy, and they picked a weekend at your granddad's to let everyone know. She must have been about four months along because she was just starting to show." Emily paused and began pacing.

"How could we have been so blind all these years?" she asked as she wrung her hands. "We were all out in the yard. Ethan and your dad were helping Grandpa in the barn. Joyce was taking them a pitcher of lemonade when I heard her scream. By the time I got to the barn, Tucker was standing there in the doorway and the others were lying on the ground. He had pulled the handle on the loft and dropped a ton of hay on his mother. Roger, Ethan, and Grandpa were up in the loft. They fell through the floor when it dropped out from under them."

Emily looked over at her husband. "When we got the hay off them, we saw that your dad had been stabbed by a pitchfork, Ethan's leg was broken from the fall, and Joyce ended up losing her babies. They had just found out she was carrying twins. The fall broke your grandfather's back. He ended up in a wheelchair for the next two years." Emily buried her face in her hands for a moment, and then looked at her son. "At the time we thought it had been an accident, but now we know it wasn't. Tucker tried to kill his parents."

Cole shook his head. He had only vague memories of the incident. Like everyone else, he'd thought it had been an accident. "So you agree with Sam? You think he'll take them back to the farm?" Cole asked.

Roger nodded. "The farm is about the only place I can think of that he knows well and is comfortable in.

Over the last ten years when we visit we've noticed that little things have changed. At first we thought someone was living there, and then about five years ago we found out it was Tucker."

"How did you find out?" Sam asked.

"Joyce noticed one of her father's chess sets was missing. She was devastated because Tucker had been fond of that particular set. When we searched the rest of the house she found it hidden under the bed in Tucker's old room. She left him a note that day, and when we went back a couple of weeks later the note was gone," Roger told them.

"Tell them what happened to the chess set," Emily demanded.

"Tucker had destroyed the pieces and hacked up the board. It had been a beautiful chess set until he destroyed it."

"Why did he destroy it?" Sam wanted to know.

Emily looked at him. "Because Joyce told him that he could have it. Her note said that because he got so much pleasure from the chess set, she wanted him to keep it."

"I don't understand," Sam said.

Emily looked at her husband before she continued with the rest of her story. "Tucker destroyed it because it represented a fond memory of his childhood and because it was a gift from his mother. He left her a note, along with a knife driven into the black queen. The note said that he didn't want anything from anyone who would treat their son the way they had treated him. He blamed them for what happened in his life after the incident in school. Joyce and Ethan were going to make him take responsibility for throwing acid in that poor boy's face.

"Now he's got his parents and his two brothers, and God only knows what's going to happen to them," Emily told them.

"Can you get to the farm and stop him?" Roger asked Cole. Cole looked at Sam and shook his head.

"He knows the river too well. We have to wait until daylight to start out. He'd be there long before then," Cole explained to his parents.

"He's traveling by boat?" Roger asked.

Cole nodded. "We thought we had him, but he slipped past us a day or so ago."

"We had him at the farm earlier today, but he managed to get away from us then too, didn't he?" Sam pointed out.

Cole shot Sam a dirty look. He hadn't wanted to be reminded about that, and he certainly didn't want his parents to know what he'd done.

"Why can't you travel at night by boat?" Roger asked.

"We don't know the river well enough," Sam told him. "We could drive, if we could borrow your car."

"I travel up and down the river all the time. I could take you back upriver," Roger volunteered. "If he's on the water, that would be your best chance of catching him. If you drive, you might beat him to the farm, but you'll miss the chance to catch him without putting anyone else at risk. If his family is with him, he might be willing to leave them unharmed in order to escape."

Cole raised his eyebrows and looked at Sam. "It makes sense. If we give him too much time to plan his next move, he won't hesitate to slit their throats. Besides, he wouldn't expect us to travel at night. We could be there shortly after he docks."

Sam nodded. "Let's go, then. I want to get there before anything happens to Wyatt."

"Who's Wyatt?" Emily asked as they headed out the front door.

"Wyatt is my six-year-old son who your nephew took hostage a few days ago. He's one of the reasons I'm here," Sam told her.

"What is the other reason?" Emily asked.

"Tucker murdered my wife almost three weeks ago."

Emily's eyes widened in shock. Now she had more reason to be afraid for her sister's family.

When they all got back to the boat, Sam noticed something different about the vessel. He swore as the others noticed the same thing he just had. The boat was listing to one side. Tucker had rammed the side of the boat, damaging the hull's integrity. There was no way they could go anywhere in this boat. They had just missed him again.

Sam looked over at Roger. "You wouldn't happen to have another boat, would you?"

Roger nodded. "As a matter of fact, I do. It's only a pontoon, but it will get us to where we have to go."

"Where is it?" Sam asked.

"Why don't we go get it, and Cole and Emily can

wait here?" Roger suggested. Cole nodded his agreement and watched as Sam and his father left the dock.

Emily folded her arms closer to her chest. The evening air had a chill that had nothing to do with the weather. "What's going to happen?" she asked her son. "To Tucker, I mean."

Cole looked out at the river rather than at his mother. He didn't want to be the one to answer her question. He didn't want to tell her that he might have to kill his cousin.

"Did he really kill that man's wife?" Emily finally asked.

Cole nodded. "Her name was Chloe. Tucker murdered her just to get Sam to come after him. He wanted Sam because he decided that Sam was the best he could find."

"The best *what* he could find?" Emily asked.

Cole looked at his mother. "The best cop, he claims. You see, no one has been able to catch him all these years, and Tucker decided to make Sam come after him by killing Sam's wife and taking his son hostage. This gives Sam a motive to keep coming after Tucker until he finally catches him. At least that's what Tucker told Sam yesterday."

Emily gasped. "Oh my gracious."

Cole nodded and looked back at the river. "We may never know just how many others Tucker has killed over the years. We know of at least seven women and three men, maybe more."

"He killed men too?"

"He finds someone that has something he wants, and he kills them and takes over their lives," Cole told her. "He's done that at least three times that we know about. He has assumed at least three different identities in the last year. One of the men was a boat salesman from New Orleans. Another was a computer troubleshooter from Myrtle Grove, Louisiana. At the farm we found more than one other form of identity. We haven't had time to check on the third man and the others yet."

"Why would he do something like this?" Emily asked.

Cole shrugged. It was hard to say why anybody did anything. Tucker had gotten very good at hiding from the law, and everyone else, for that matter.

An hour later they were on their way up the river. Emily was strangely quiet, and Roger kept looking at her. He could only imagine what she had found out while they were gone.

The river was calm and serene that night, and the gentle rocking of the boat had clearly made Sam tired, as he'd fallen asleep shortly after they'd left the dock.

"What on earth did you tell your mother?" Roger asked his son after noticing that Emily had also fallen asleep and they were the only ones awake.

Cole shrugged. "She asked if Tucker had really killed Sam's wife. I told her that he had."

Roger was quiet for a moment. He knew what family meant to his wife, what it meant to him, and he couldn't think of one reason why this was happening to his family. "What else did she ask about?"

"She wanted to know why Tucker was doing all this," Cole told him.

"What did you tell her?"

Cole shrugged. "What *could* I tell her? I don't know the reasons myself."

Roger knew his son very well, and he knew that there was something else he wanted to talk about but didn't know how to bring it up. "Something else bothering you?" he asked Cole.

Cole looked at his dad and then out at the water. "I was just wondering what I ever did to Tucker to really tick him off. He said that we have issues to settle, but I can't think of what they are. I mean, we had almost the same things growing up. Whatever I got, he did too."

"Maybe that was the problem." Roger thought out loud. "We were so used to you two being thought of as twins that we treated you boys like brothers, and you weren't. You were two totally different boys, and yet we treated you the same."

Cole nodded. "I thought that too, at first. Maybe he resented being treated like my brother, but he never said so. If something is bothering you, you speak up and tell someone about your feelings. Tucker never did that. At least, I don't remember him doing that."

Roger didn't speak for a moment. "Maybe he did, but we just didn't listen."

"You can beat yourself up about it all you want, but nobody did anything to make him a killer. He had the choice to make, and he made it a long time ago," Cole told his father.

"He's still your cousin," Roger pointed out.

"By birth he's family, but he stopped being my cousin a long time ago. Anybody can accidentally hurt someone one time, but Tucker goes out of his way to inflict pain and misery on people. He didn't *have* to keep on killing—he *chose* to. He got good at it. He took pride in his work. He stopped thinking about us as family years ago. Now he's just another monster who has to be stopped." Cole looked at his father. "Sam won't let him get away this time. By tomorrow, Tucker will either be dead or going to jail for the rest of his life, and I can't really see him going to jail—not after all this."

Roger was quiet as he considered Cole's words. He knew his son was right. Tucker had to be stopped.

An hour later, they had reached the halfway point. Sam woke up briefly, and after taking his phone off his belt, turned over and went back to sleep. Emily was still sleeping, and Cole had taken over steering the boat while Roger took a nap. Cole didn't mind traveling at night. His dad had explained what to look for and what to steer clear of and told him to just go steady and slow, and he was doing just that.

Cole was yawning when he heard Sam's phone ring. He grabbed it quickly and answered it. He heard Tucker's voice call out Sam's name. "What do you want?" he asked his cousin.

Tucker paused and then began laughing. "So, he didn't kill you? That's good. I thought he would have by now."

"Thanks, I think. Maybe I'm more use to him alive than dead," Cole told his cousin.

"So, where is he?"

"He's not here at the moment. Is there anything I can do for you?" Cole asked.

"You aren't the one I want right now," Tucker told him.

"That's too bad, because I'm the only one you've got."

"Are you sure about that?" Tucker asked slyly.

"Are you talking about your parents and your brothers?" Cole remarked.

"You followed me back home, didn't you?" Tucker laughed. "Did you like the surprise I left you at the boat?"

"That wasn't very nice, you know," Cole shot back.

"Hey, we have to do what we have to do. I didn't want you guys to catch up with me, so I had to try to stop you."

"We will catch up with you. You know that. It's just a matter of time," Cole stated bluntly.

"Maybe, but will you get here in time? Ticktock, ticktock."

"Why are you doing this?" Cole finally had to ask.

"This was something I've been planning a long time, but I had other things to do until now. When this is all over, I'm going to disappear, and to do that I needed enough money to live on. Don't worry, Cousin, your time is coming and you won't even see me until it's too late."

"You won't get the chance," Cole told him. "Tomorrow is your day of reckoning."

Tucker just laughed. "Well, it will be for some of us, but when the sun goes down we'll see who's alive and who isn't."

"You don't scare me, Tucker. Not anymore," Cole told him.

"You were scared earlier today, and I didn't even have my knife out," Tucker reminded him. "You almost wet your pants."

"That was before I realized something about you."

"Oh, and what did you realize?"

"That you're nothing but a coward. You hide what you really are by stealing other people's lives. You hurt the people that love you the most and have turned your back on anything decent because you're just too afraid to try."

Tucker was silent for a long minute. "If that's what you believe, then it isn't any wonder you haven't caught me yet."

"You can fool most of the people you come across, but you can't fool me. I know you too well," Cole reminded him.

"You don't know me at all, if you think I'm a coward," Tucker grumbled. "I'm not afraid of you or anyone else, and I'm not afraid to die either. If either of us is a coward, it's you. You never stood up for me when we were kids. You never once protected me against anyone."

"You mean I wouldn't lie for you, or take a punishment that was yours. Your actions caused the most damage, so why should I protect you from that?"

"All I ever wanted was for someone to show me that they thought I mattered. I wasn't just a pale shadow of you. You helped create what I became." Tucker was angry and clearly didn't care if Cole knew it.

"No, you did that all by yourself," Cole told him quietly.

"What do you mean?"

"You made the choice to kill, not me. You made the choice to steal other people's lives, not me," Cole reminded him. "You're the one who turned your back on the rest of us—no one else did it for you."

"I'm going to enjoy killing you tomorrow. We'll see then who begs for his life," Tucker told him.

Cole quietly closed the phone, cutting the connection. He didn't know if he could take any more of Tucker's wild accusations.

Tucker watched as Cole continued to steer the pontoon toward Hannibal. Cole wasn't paying attention to the river behind him or he would have seen Tucker following in his wake as he passed yet another river island. Cole didn't see the houseboat moored behind the island, the same boat they had been looking for since they left Mississippi. Its black hull blended so well with the night sky that you could barely see it in the shadow of the island.

Tucker reached for the pontoon's ladder and quietly hauled himself out of the water. It only took him seconds to see where everyone was. By pure chance, he had pulled his boat off the river just an hour ago. When he hung up the phone, he realized they were passing right in front of him. Before the boat completely passed his island, Tucker didn't think about what he was going to do—he just dove into the water. It didn't take him too long to catch up with the boat, and a few minutes later he boarded it. When he saw that everyone was sleeping except for Cole, Tucker smiled.

He reached for the knife on his belt. Using the ivory handle that had worked so well as a club earlier, he walked up behind Cole and hit him. Cole groaned and slumped forward. The boat rocked a bit, then settled into a nice steady ride. Tucker grabbed his cousin's hand and sliced it open just enough to make it bleed profusely. He wanted everyone to think Cole was seriously injured. He smeared the blood around the steering wheel and dribbled it along the floor of the boat. Then he shut off the motor and broke the key. He didn't want whoever woke up first to catch up to them too quickly. His cousin had made him angry, and he would make him pay for what he had said, but he wanted to have a little fun with him first.

Tucker grabbed Cole by the arms and dragged him to the back of the boat. It would serve him right if he just dumped his body in the water and let him drown, but Tucker wasn't feeling generous tonight. Cole had said some nasty things to him, and he wanted him to see death coming.

Tucker and Cole made very little noise as they slipped down off the boat into the water. Tucker grabbed his cousin under the chin and swam him back to the island.

He was winded and exhausted by the time they got there, and when he pulled Cole out of the water, Tucker slugged him in the face. He knew Cole wouldn't feel it now, but when he woke up it would hurt. For the moment, that would have to be enough. Tomorrow would be the real test. It would all depend on who was still alive when the sun went down.

Chapter Twelve

It wasn't quite daylight when Sam woke up. The boat was still moving, but it wasn't moving correctly. He sat up and looked around. Roger and Emily were still sleeping, but where was Cole? That's when he realized the engine wasn't running and they were drifting.

Sam looked out at the river. They were headed for the bank, and the current was carrying them out of the main channel. Sam jumped up and tried to restart the engine. That's when he noticed the broken key. He swore. He tried the steering wheel, but that didn't work either. Looking over at Roger and Emily, he found them awake and looking back at him. He told Roger, "Someone shut off the engine and broke the key. Is there any other way to restart the engine?"

Roger jumped up and joined him. Squatting down, he had a look at the ignition. There was just enough of the key left to try to turn over the engine. After fiddling around with it for a moment, Roger made the motor roar to life.

Once he made the correction, they were back on course, and he began looking around the small craft. His fingers were sticky, and when he raised them to see what was on them, he and Sam saw the blood. He slowed the boat and, putting it in neutral, let it drift while he looked around more closely. That's when he saw the trail of blood leading to the back of the boat.

Sam found his phone up on the dash of the boat. He had a text message. Punching in his code, he read the message.

Emily had fear and concern in her eyes and Roger was looking around to pinpoint their location. "Where's Cole?" Emily asked.

"Tucker's got him," Sam told her.

"What? How?" Roger blustered. "He was driving the boat last night."

"I didn't hear a thing," Sam told them. "All I have to go on is this message." He handed the phone to Emily and watched as she handed it to Roger. Her eyes filled with tears.

"Do you have any idea where we are?" Sam asked the older man.

Roger gave the phone back to Emily and stood up to have a good look around. He turned back to Sam and nodded. "We're only about fifteen miles south of the farm. We should get there in about forty minutes or so." He ran his fingers through his hair. "How did Tucker get his hands on Cole? He was so far in front of us."

Sam shrugged. "I wish I knew. All we can hope for is that Cole is okay and we meet up with them at the farm." Sam stopped to look at Roger. "Is there a place nearby that can hide a boat like Tucker's and still give him access to land?"

Roger thought for a moment and then nodded. "Sure, other than the dock, there is a small inlet near the caves. It's out of the way, and you can't see it from the river. You have to know where it is in order to get to it, but the boys used to go fishing there when they were younger."

"Can you get us to the inlet? I have a feeling that's where we'll find the boat Tucker is using," Sam told them.

Roger started up the engine and steered the pontoon back out into the middle of the river. As they got closer to the farm, he steered the boat over to the right side of the river and up into the backwater. Turning the corner, they found the black houseboat. They also saw another one moored in the inlet.

Sam sat forward and surveyed the scene. "Okay, let's go back to the dock. We know where they are now, but they don't know where we are. Let's keep it that way for at least a little while."

Roger reversed the pontoon out of the backwater and onto the main channel of the river. They tethered the pontoon at the dock for the farm. Roger turned to Sam. "What are your plans?"

Sam was busy gathering his things. He looked up at Roger. "I want you to take your wife away from here. If things go wrong, I don't want Tucker to get either of you. Go, find the nearest police department, and have them call this number and talk to Alec Hunter. He's my partner in New Orleans and he'll tell them what they need to know. Don't come back here. Tell the police Tucker will likely kill anyone he sees, and I don't want any more policemen caught unaware in his line of fire."

"There's no way the police will make it down here in time to help you," Emily said.

Sam smiled. "I know. But I don't know what today will bring. I'll have whoever survives give the nearest police station a call."

Emily nodded. "Please take care of yourself, and try to get the others out alive."

"Don't worry, that's the first thing on my list of things to do today."

Sam watched as Emily and Roger made their way back out to the river. He turned to the path leading to the barn and the house beyond. He didn't know where anyone was, so he stayed out of sight as long as he could. The brush he struggled through was dry and scratched at his clothes. He got within fifty feet of the barn before he ran out of cover.

He didn't have a choice. He broke cover to run across the road. The tall grasses there hid him well almost the entire rest of the way. He stopped to see if he could hear any sounds coming from the barn.

Looking around, he noticed that something was lying in the grass just ahead of him. Moving in closer to see what it was, he found the first dead body. It was Jasper Wiley. Tucker had slit his throat. *So much for friendship,* Sam thought.

The blood on Jasper's body was still warm and sticky, so Sam concluded that Wiley had just been murdered. Sam pulled out his weapon and snuck closer to the barn.

Roger and Cole had thought that this was where Tucker planned to kill his family, but Sam had no doubt that they were wrong.

Sam saw a way to get inside without using the door. There was a broken window. He got closer to the window and peeked through. The small room was dark and smelled of old leather. This must have been the tack room. Sam hoisted himself up on the sill and slipped inside. He waited for his eyes to adjust to the dim surroundings before he moved to the door.

He peeked through the slats of the door and listened for any sounds from outside the room. He saw a young boy lying on the ground on the main floor of the barn. The boy was tied up and appeared to be unconscious. Sam couldn't see anyone else from this angle.

He took a chance and slid his hand down the door to find the handle. Carefully turning the old knob, he heard the door protesting the motion after being stationary for so long. Sam waited for any movement outside the room, but when he didn't hear anything he slipped out of the tack room and into the main part of the barn.

He flattened himself against the wall and crept toward the end of the wall. Taking a deep breath, he lifted his gun to firing position and carefully peeked around the corner of the wall. He saw three more bodies lying in the same way as the first. All were bound and unconscious.

He checked for signs of breathing and was glad to see that they were.

Sam cocked his head and listened for any other signs of Tucker and Cole. He hadn't yet seen Wyatt, so he was hoping that he was with the other two men. He didn't hear anything, so he moved a little closer.

When he was nearer to the man he understood to be Ethan, he saw that Ethan was looking straight at him. Ethan didn't dare move, but he looked upward toward the loft and Sam understood what he was trying to tell him. Tucker was up in the loft. Sam fished out his pocket knife and slid it over to Ethan. Then he put his finger over his mouth and told Ethan to be quiet. Ethan nodded and picked up the knife and began sawing at the ropes around his wrists.

Sam found the ladder to the loft, and taking one step at a time, made his way up. Peeking his head over the floor of the loft, he finally saw Cole and Tucker.

Cole was on his knees with his hands tied behind his back. They were both facing away, so they didn't notice Sam. Tucker was pushing the hay around Cole. Sam looked around the loft again. He didn't see any sign of Wyatt.

"So, what are you going to do now, Cousin?" he heard Cole ask.

"I have to get ready for your friend Sam," Tucker replied.

Sam heard someone sneeze and he recognized the sound. Wyatt was there, and he was still alive. Sam almost jumped right up at that moment, but knew he couldn't.

"What are you going to do?" Cole asked again.

Sam peeked over the edge of the loft and saw Tucker turn and smile. Cole was surrounded by hay up to his chest. A path had been cleared in a circle all the way around him. Sam feared that when the time came, Tucker was going to burn his cousin alive.

He had to distract him, but how? Sam looked down at Tucker's family. Ethan had cut through his and Joyce's ropes, but the boys' were still bound. He caught Ethan's eye and motioned for him to get his family out of the barn.

Ethan nodded, and he and Joyce each carried or dragged their sons clear of the barn. Taking a deep breath, Sam raised his weapon to his chest and called out Tucker's name. "Tucker Briggs, you are under arrest."

Tucker laughed out loud. He looked over at Cole. "Guess who's here and ready to play?" He looked over to the top of the ladder leading up to the loft. "Why don't you join us, Sam?" he called out.

Sam climbed up to the loft. There at the edge of the loft, in the middle of the double doors leading to the outside, stood Tucker and Wyatt.

Sam could see that Wyatt's hands were tied behind his back. Tucker had hold of his shirt and held him almost off the ground.

Sam knew that one step backward was all it would

take to send them both crashing down a twenty-foot drop to the ground outside. Tucker had an unholy gleam in his black eyes. Sam could see that Wyatt was scared to death. Who wouldn't be, with a seven-inch knife blade at their throat, and being dangled so close to a ledge?

"Well, I see you saved the good people who are supposed to be my family," Tucker said. "By the way, why don't you lose your gun? I would hate to have to drop your son out the window."

Sam slowly lowered his weapon to the floor.

"Let the boy go, Tucker, or you won't have a chance in the world of getting out of this barn alive," Sam told him as he watched his son struggle to keep his feet on the ground.

Tucker threw his head back and laughed. "You don't scare me, fool. Don't you know by now what I was planning? Hasn't it sunk in yet why I let you follow me? I explained my reason to you that night out on the river. Didn't you believe me?"

Sam frowned. He wasn't sure what Tucker meant. He tried to think about what was said that night. He remembered that Tucker had told him that he might be the only one who could stop him. Sam decided to stall for more time to figure out what to do. "Tell me one thing, will you? Why did you kill all those people?"

Tucker looked sad for a moment, as if he really cared, and then his eyes hardened as he began to finally tell his side of the family saga. "Do you know what it's like to be a disappointment to your parents, almost from the first day of your life? To grow up hearing the words 'Why can't you be as clever as your cousin?' or 'Come on, Tucker, Cole walked at thirteen months, so why can't you?' You know, some kids might fight harder to please their parents, but I didn't. I knew that no matter what I did, I could never be as clever or as smart as my cousin Cole.

"Cole knew it too, and while we were younger it didn't seem to matter. We were more like twins than real twins ever were. Then something happened to change all that. Cole betrayed me." Tucker paused at the fresh memories of the betrayal.

"Is this about the bully in school teasing you about your mother being pregnant?" Sam asked.

Tucker laughed. "No, but I am surprised he told you about that. Cole doesn't like to admit to anyone that he isn't perfect."

Tucker began pacing back and forth in front of the window, dragging Wyatt with him. Sam's heart leaped to his throat as he watched his son struggling to keep up with Tucker.

"No, this happened much earlier." Tucker sneered at Cole. "We were about six, I guess, when my dad said I could have a puppy, if I was the one to take care of it. I was so happy. I was finally going to have something Cole couldn't. Cole wasn't allowed to have pets, but my dad said *I* could have a dog. We went to the pet store and I picked out the dog I wanted. It was a golden cocker spaniel, and I called her Lady, after *Lady and the Tramp*.

"I took care of her the best I could, until the day I came home and found Cole playing with her." Tucker's voice hardened.

"Somebody had to play with her—you never did," Cole interjected.

"You had no business being around her. She was *my* dog." Tucker shouted. "She was the only thing I could have that you couldn't, and you managed to steal her love away from me."

"No, I didn't," Cole said quietly. "All I did was play with her when you didn't. I was glad that you had her."

"What happened next?" Sam asked. He sensed that Tucker was getting too caught up in the story to think about his hostage, Wyatt.

Cole took over telling the story. "Tucker got so mad at me that he killed the dog. He called her over to him, and she went willingly. Then he twisted her neck so hard he broke it. Then he told me, 'Now play with that.' "

"My mother came in just about then," Tucker stated. "When she saw the dog, she asked what happened. I told her that Cole killed Lady, but she didn't believe me. She never believed me. She turned to Cole for the explanation. At first Cole wouldn't tell her. He wouldn't say a word, but then his mother came in and asked what happened, and the little whiner told them what I'd done. He betrayed me."

"You had just killed a dog in front of me. We were only six at the time, but I knew why you did it. Did you think you were the only one to feel the pressure of be-ing an only child in a family of twins?" Cole asked. "I had those feeling too. People were always mistaking us for twins, but that day I was glad we weren't. I hated you for killing Lady, and I was glad when you got in trouble for it."

Tucker looked at Cole in a new light. "You told them that I killed Lady because I didn't like her anymore. You told them that I told you that she was too much trouble."

"I was mad at you. I was a *kid*. What you did traumatized me. I had nightmares about it for the longest time," Cole defended himself.

"So did I, Cousin." Tucker reminded him. "You knew I loved that dog. You of all people knew how I felt about her."

"How could you kill her just because I was playing with her?" Cole asked. "She was so happy to see you. She came to you willingly. You changed that day. I saw it but didn't understand at the time. It was like you shut off part of your brain. You weren't the same." Cole paused. "Did you purposely cause the accident that broke Grandpa's back and made your mom lose her babies?"

Tucker scowled. "What do you think?"

Cole shook his head. "I always thought it was an accident."

"Everyone was laughing at me and telling me how having new babies in the house would really suck. John was the worst, but I got even with him that day in chemistry class. I could feel the rage building inside me, and then I couldn't take it anymore. I had to hurt somebody,

so I grabbed the rope and pulled as hard as I could."
That one incident had been the first step toward what he
had become.

"Now what?" Cole asked.

"I won't let you take me in," Tucker told them.

"You need help," Cole started to tell him.

Tucker laughed out loud. "You think I'm crazy? Is
that what you've been telling yourself all these years?"
He grabbed Wyatt's shirt and pulled him closer. Lifting
him off the ground, Tucker whispered loudly in his ear.
"Is that what you think, boy? You think that I'm crazy?
Huh? Am I a crazy man?"

Wyatt shook his head. His eyes were round with fear,
and his feet were feeling for something solid to rest on.
Sweat beaded his forehead and Sam grew alarmed. "No,
sir," Wyatt whispered.

"Please don't hurt him. He's just a kid," Sam begged,
as the tension mounted in the hayloft. Tucker was holding all the cards, and Sam and Cole knew it. Sam could
tell from the look in his eyes that Tucker wouldn't hesitate to kill his son.

"Why did you carve a headstone in their backs?"
Cole asked, trying to divert Tucker's attention from the
child.

"I knew that was the one thing you and only you
would know about. How long did it take you to figure
out what the design meant?" Tucker scoffed.

"I figured out what the design was on your third victim, Sarah Gold," Cole told him.

Tucker nodded. He remembered Sarah. The look on

his face said that he remembered them all. "You know what you have to do to stop me, don't you?"

Cole shook his head. "I won't kill you."

Tucker smiled as he looked at Sam. "How about you, Dad? Are you going to kill me, or let me walk away with your kid again?"

Sam looked at his gun and then back at Tucker. Tucker could see the want on Sam's face.

"If you don't, I'll use this boy as a shield to get away from you, and I will kill again," Tucker told them.

When Sam didn't comment, Tucker sneered. "It didn't bother me at first—killing them, I mean," Tucker began. "I would pick someone I felt had nothing left to lose and I would just slit their throat. Then something happened. Around the fourth or fifth person I killed, I started to enjoy the whole process. It became something I craved. I needed to feel the excitement of looking for my next victim. It gave me something to look forward to. I would find just the right one, and I would watch them go about their lives. The waiting was the best part because I grew to appreciate what I was waiting for. I waited until the rage inside me was so strong I needed to feel the release only a murder could bring. I loved to hear them scream as I carved their own headstone into their skin. I can still hear the screams when I think about the way they all died. That's why I carved them while they were still alive."

Sam shook his head. "How many victims didn't we find?"

Tucker just smiled. "Well, now, that would all depend on when you started looking, wouldn't it?"

From out of nowhere came a gunshot. Cole looked at his cousin. He had a funny look on his face. Sam turned around with his gun drawn.

At the top of the loft steps stood Ethan Davidson, the gun in his hand pointed at his oldest son.

Chapter Thirteen

Sam and Cole turned to see Tucker crumple to the ground. He had let Wyatt go and had fallen on top of the boy.

Sam scrambled over to them. He pushed Tucker's body off his son and pulled Wyatt into his arms. Wyatt was crying, and Sam grabbed the knife from Tucker's limp hand and used it to cut through the tape that bound Wyatt's hands.

Wyatt threw his arms around his dad's neck. Lifting him away from Tucker, Sam carried the boy over to where Ethan was helping to free Cole.

Ethan looked at his son and shook his head. "I had to put an end to this madness. I couldn't believe what he was saying. That monster wasn't the son I raised. I loved Tucker once, and I guess a part of me still does, but I couldn't let him go free. I couldn't let you allow him to escape with the boy. God knows he would have murdered that child just like he did all the others."

Cole reached out to his uncle. "I'm sorry, Uncle Ethan.

I don't think he wanted to escape this time. He chose the place, and he knew in his heart that he wasn't going to get out of here alive."

Ethan looked at Cole. "Did he really mean all those awful things he said . . . about how he enjoyed killing all those people?"

Cole shook his head as he looked over at his cousin's body. "I don't know. I can't imagine."

Ethan sighed. "I always knew there was something wrong with Tucker, but I never imagined anything like that."

Ethan and Cole looked at Tucker one last time. Tucker was sprawled out on the hay. His life was ended, along with his need to kill.

They joined the rest of Ethan's family outside the barn. Joyce and the boys were glad to see Cole and the others, but Joyce was looking for the one person who was missing. She looked at her husband, and when he shook his head, she turned away and began crying. She knew that her oldest son was dead.

Sam felt relief for the first time in weeks. He had his son back and the killer was dead. He reached for his phone and dialed 911. He spoke to the operator and asked that the nearest police department be dispatched to the farm. Then he looked at his son.

Wyatt looked up at his dad and smiled. Sam picked him up and held him close. The worry he'd felt for so long melted away as his son's arms reached around his neck. He felt almost whole, and he knew he never wanted to be apart from his son again.

Cole watched the reunion and smiled. It felt good to see something worthwhile come out of all this misery. He hated to break up the moment, but asked, "Sam, where are my parents?"

Sam tossed him the phone. "I called the local cop shop, and they should be here any time now."

Cole let go a huge sigh of relief when he heard the first of the sirens wailing in the distance. His parents were on their way back, and this mess was finally over. He felt a degree of sadness for his aunt and uncle, and as he looked over at them he wasn't sure what to say.

Joyce stood in Ethan's arms, her tears drying, and when she saw Cole join them, she obviously didn't know what to say either. "I'm so sorry," she finally told him.

Cole shook his head. "Sorry for what?"

Joyce closed her eyes. "He was still my son. I heard some of what he said up there. I couldn't believe it, but I know it was true."

"You can't blame yourself for what he did," Cole told his aunt. "Tucker chose his own path in life. You had nothing to do with what he became any more than I did."

They all turned their attention to the front of the yard as several police cars pulled into the driveway with their lights flashing and sirens wailing. One by one the sirens died, but the lights were left on as the police officers emerged from their vehicles and headed toward the group.

One officer introduced himself as John Sanders. Sam stepped forward to handle any questions. "I'm Detective Sam Sebastian from New Orleans."

Sanders held out his hand and as they shook, he said, "You're kind of a long way from home, aren't you, Mr. Sebastian?"

"We were trailing a serial killer and this is where he brought us," Sam said.

"What happened here today?" he asked.

"Tucker Briggs kidnapped his parents, my son, and his own cousin, and brought them here to kill them. I've been following him for a week, since he kidnapped my son and murdered several other people, including three police officers in Louisiana."

John raised an eyebrow. "And where exactly is Tucker Briggs right now?"

Sam nodded toward the barn. "His body is up in the hayloft. You'll find a bullet in his chest."

John called out to one of the other cops standing in the yard. He told him to go check out the barn loft for a dead body. Turning back to Sam he asked, "Who shot him?"

Ethan took a step forward and said, "I did."

John looked at Sam for a long minute and then turned to Ethan. "And you are?"

"I'm Tucker's father. I shot him before he could hurt anyone else."

Before he could comment, John was called to the barn door by the officer he'd sent in to find the body. They talked for a few minute, and then John rejoined the group. He was looking at Sam when he asked, "What is going on here?"

Sam frowned. "What are you talking about?"

John looked back at the barn. "There is no dead body in that hayloft. The barn is empty."

Sam looked at Cole, and Cole returned the look. Fear and dread filled him. Sam turned to Ethan. "Keep Wyatt with you and stay here. Don't leave or wander away from the lights."

"Where do you think you're going?" John stated as he tried to stop Sam. He reached out and grabbed Sam's arm.

Sam jerked his arm out of his grasp and turned around to head for the barn. He glared at the other man. He was about to give him a piece of his mind when Ethan interrupted him.

"What's happening?" Ethan wanted to know.

Sam glared at the other officer for a moment, then turned to look at the barn. Glancing back at Ethan, he informed him, "They can't find Tucker's body."

"What?" Ethan called out, shaken. He too looked at the barn. "But I saw him fall after I shot him. He has to be there."

Sam didn't say anything. He and Cole headed for the barn. They slowly climbed the ladder to the loft. They both had their guns ready, but when they peeked over the top of the ladder, they found the hayloft empty. Sam scrambled over the ladder and walked over to where Tucker's body had fallen. He pushed the hay around and couldn't even find a bloodstain.

Cole was moving around the perimeter of the loft looking for any sign of disturbance. He didn't find any. He rejoined Sam. "What do you think happened?"

Sam looked at the spot where he'd last seen Tucker. "I think your cousin is a very clever man," he said.

"What are you talking about?"

Sam looked at Cole. "He was counting on one of us shooting him. A cop shoots for the heart, nine times out of ten. Tucker was counting on that. He wasn't expecting his own father to shoot him, but lucky for him, Ethan took a chest shot."

"How was that lucky? It killed him, didn't it?"

Sam shook his head and squatted down to pick up a piece of link out of the hay. He held it up for Cole to see. "Tucker was wearing a vest. The bullet only stunned him. After we left, he just got up and walked away."

"Now what do we do?"

Sam walked over to the double-wide window at the end of the loft. Looking out at the scene below him, he thought for a moment. Turning back to Cole, he told the other man, "He's still here. He hasn't had time enough to get too far away. We have to find him before he gets away."

"Let's do it," Cole said.

"First we have to get everyone else out of here. I won't put them in danger," Sam said as he formulated a plan.

Cole nodded and headed for the ladder. When they joined the others, Cole found that his parents had joined the group.

Sam looked at them and stated, "He's alive and he's out there somewhere, hiding."

Ethan shook his head. "But I shot him. I saw him

fall." Tears of regret welled in his eyes. This whole affair had left him befuddled and bewildered.

"He was wearing a bulletproof vest. He waited until we were gone, and then he just got up and walked away," Sam told them. He looked at John Sanders. "As officer on the scene, I am instituting my command. I need you and your people to set up a perimeter. Cole and I will look for Tucker and try to bring him in. I will also need all civilians moved out of harm's way."

Sanders nodded and, barking orders, turned back to his officers.

"I have enough men to help you search the farm," John said, turning back toward Sam.

Sam shook his head. "How many?"

John looked around. "Maybe around a dozen—once we've secured the location."

"Okay, but I have to warn you, you have no idea what this man is like. He'll kill each and every one of your men without hesitation if you put them in his way." Sam's words slammed his message home to everyone in the group. Joyce groaned in fear, and Sam turned to the others. "I need some officers to get everyone you can on Roger's boat and take them out to the middle of the river, where they'll be safe. Don't bring them back here until this is all over. Do you hear me?"

One of the cops moved forward and herded the group toward the river and the safety of Roger's boat.

Sam turned to John Sanders. "Are you ready?"

"We've got you covered—you apprehend him," John told him.

"Good. Get your men in place and let us do our job," Sam told him. He looked at Cole and asked, "Are you ready?"

Cole pulled out his gun and nodded.

They began at the barn. Sam hoped to pick up Tucker's trail, but if he left one, it wasn't in the tall grass around the barn. They couldn't even find any footprints. Sam turned to Cole and asked, "Is there any other way out of the barn?"

Cole thought for a moment but shook his head. "Not that I know of, but then I haven't been back here in years."

"Let's go back up to the loft. Maybe we'll find one," Sam suggested. Making his way back up to the loft, Sam looked around. The area didn't look disturbed, but they had to be overlooking something. He took one side and motioned for Cole to take the other.

Moving the hay around was tedious, but Sam wasn't leaving this barn until he found out how Tucker had gotten out. He moved the loose hay with his foot and checked everywhere he could. Cole was doing the same on the other side of the room.

"Sam, I found it!" Cole shouted. Sam turned and rushed over to where Cole was standing. Cole had uncovered a trapdoor hidden by the loose hay.

Sam reached down and grabbed the metal ring and pulled the door up. It led to another part of the lower barn. Sam looked at Cole. "I'm going down. You go around by the ladder and come down that way. I'll meet you there. If Tucker is still in the barn, I don't want to miss him."

Cole nodded and turned to leave. Sam looked into the darkness below him. He wasn't sure what, if anything, was down there, but he wasn't going to take any chances. He lowered himself and jumped the last few feet.

He crouched low and looked around. This part of the barn was in shadows, as all the windows and the big double doors were closed. When it had been a working barn, this must have been where the cows were milked. Sam eased himself over to the wall and began circling around it. He couldn't see very well in the dim light, but by the time he came full circle, he was sure that if Tucker had been here, he wasn't anymore.

He joined Cole in the main part of the barn. "Did you find anything?" he asked Cole.

Cole shook his head. "I checked the other room, and there was nothing there."

"Then I guess the only other way he got out was through the back. Come on." Sam motioned for Cole to follow him.

Sam and Cole went to the door in the back of the barn. With their guns ready, they slid the door open. Outside they found what they were looking for: a trail they could follow. Someone had forced their way through the tall grass. Following the trail, they found a bulletproof vest about fifty feet from the barn. Sam picked up the vest and checked for a bullet. He found one.

Sam looked at Cole and pointed out the bullet hole. Cole looked away. Tucker had outwitted them every step of the way, until now.

They followed the trail to the rear of the farmhouse. Sam opened the back door, and as they made their way inside, they split up and began to search the downstairs. Room by room they searched until they met at the staircase going to the second floor.

Sam led the way upstairs. When they reached the top of the steps again they separated and each took a side of the hall. Opening every door, they found no sign of Tucker.

Cole led the way back downstairs. They had one more place to look. In the sitting room, Cole lifted the trapdoor to the caves. Before they descended, Cole warned Sam, "Be careful. We can't use any lights, so the tunnels will be dark."

Sam nodded and waited until Cole disappeared, and then he followed into the darkness. They waited until their eyes became adjusted to the surroundings before they started down the tunnel to the cave beyond. It was slow going, but they finally entered the larger cavern.

Sam went to the smaller room where they had found the camping gear. The suitcase that had been there earlier was gone. Sam rejoined Cole, and together they made their way to the cave opening.

The brightness of the sun hurt their eyes as they left the cave. Sam shaded his eyes and looked around. "How do we get back to the inlet?"

Cole grabbed Sam's arm. "It's just up around the next corner."

Sam nodded and edged his way to where the path turned right. Down below, they could see the boats,

Tucker's houseboat as well as Jasper's black one. They didn't know which boat Tucker was on, so they would have to approach carefully. Sam ducked back behind the curve of the path.

"So, how are we going to do this?" Cole asked.

Sam peeked back around the bend and watched the boats for a few minutes. He turned back to Cole. "You'll have to take one boat and I'll take the other."

Cole nodded. "We should call the river patrol. They can block the entrance to the inlet."

"Good idea—call your dad and tell him to have Sanders call it in," Sam suggested as he handed his cell phone to Cole. "Have them stop any boat that comes out of this cove."

Cole placed the call while Sam kept an eye on the boats. He couldn't see movement on either of them, but that didn't mean Tucker wasn't on one.

"My father is getting Sanders on it. He said to hold off boarding either boat for about fifteen minutes. That would give the patrol time to get here," Cole told Sam as he handed the phone back to him.

"I guess I can wait that long. He doesn't seem to be in too much of a hurry to leave anyway," Sam said.

"One thing he isn't is stupid. He wouldn't have lived this long doing what he's been doing if he was," Cole remarked. "He thinks he's safe, tucked away here. Not very many people know about this spot. I'm surprised my dad knew about it."

"I think your dad knows a great deal more than you give him credit for," Sam said.

"I never had time to thank you for saving my life back there in the barn. I was sure Tucker was going to set the whole place on fire," Cole said.

"I think that was his intention all along. He isn't crazy, you know." Sam had recognized the look in Tucker's eyes. Very few men had it, but Sam knew what that look meant—nothing but pure evil.

Cole shook his head. "I'm not so sure about that. Did you see the way he looked when he said that he began enjoying killing all those people? I've never seen anyone look like that, or tell in detail what Tucker told us today." Cole shook his head.

Sam nodded. "I have. We had a case once, where we went up against a killer. Dan Thompson was his name. We found his latest victim burning in a pile of trash. Someone called in a tip that Dan had been burning trash for the last three days in a dry season. When we responded, we found he was burning a body. We didn't have a whole lot left to process, but we did identify the body. It was Mrs. Thompson. When we asked him why he killed her, at first he said it was because he couldn't stand her nagging him all the time. After we questioned him some more, he broke down and told us the truth. He just enjoyed killing. We found out later that he had killed seven other people over as many years, and that he'd burned their bodies as well. He had that same crazy look in his eye that Tucker did."

Cole shook his head. "I never knew he hated me as much as he does, or that he blamed me for Lady's death. It just doesn't make any sense."

Sam shook his head. "That was the excuse he used to pin his problems on someone else. He wasn't sincere. He was playing you."

"How do you know that?" Cole asked.

"His reasons didn't make any sense to me, and the gleam in his eye told me he wasn't telling the truth. When he started talking about why he killed, that's when he was being honest. There was a different look in his eyes when he talked about the murders. That was the real truth speaking."

Cole was confused. "What was the truth, then?"

Sam shrugged. "He just liked to kill. Sometimes it's nothing more than that. He used your guilt to make you think differently, but he just enjoyed killing."

Sam looked at Cole. "Are you going to be able to kill him? Can you forget that you're his cousin and kill him if you have to?"

Cole nodded. "I know I can. After hearing what I heard, I don't think that will be a problem. Like I said, he stopped being my cousin a long time ago. He won't get past me this time."

Sam nodded. "Okay, it's been about fifteen minutes, so let's go. I'll take Jasper's houseboat, and you take the other one. Be quiet and be careful. If he's not on Jasper's boat, I'll meet you onboard the other."

"Same here," Cole told him.

Keeping to the brush as long as they could, Sam and Cole made their way to the dock. The black houseboat was on the left, and Tucker's boat was on the right.

Crouching low, Sam broke cover and made his way to the black boat. Cole did the same.

Each man quietly boarded his boat. Sam hoped Tucker would be aboard his. He was looking to confront the man who had killed his wife and taken his son hostage. Sam reached out and grabbed the handle for the door that led belowdecks.

Turning the handle, he opened the door slowly.

Chapter Fourteen

Tucker heard the soft thud of someone boarding the boat, and felt it rock slightly as someone stepped aboard. He listened intently as footsteps crossed the roof over his head. He had hoped for a little more time to make his escape. It had been his good luck that his father had shot him in the chest. His father could just as well have hit him in the head or shoulder. The blow had stunned him, causing him to drop like he'd actually been shot.

When he recovered from the blow to his chest, he'd found himself alone. The others had already gone down to the barnyard and he had heard every word they'd said. He had almost laughed out loud as he slipped down the trapdoor and made his way to the house. From there he'd gone directly to the cave. Collecting his things, he'd made his way to Jasper's boat.

He had decided to take Jasper's rather than his because, with a fresh paint job, Jasper's boat would be easier to pass off than his newer model. Now he was waiting for nightfall to make his escape. This cove was hidden and very few people knew about it, so he had counted on Cole not knowing about it either. When he heard the footsteps, he realized he had been wrong.

Tucker grabbed his knife and ducked down into the shadows. He waited for the door to open. Sweat beaded on his forehead and dripped down the side of his face. He watched the doorknob turn ever so slowly.

Sam hesitated before he opened the door. He could almost hear Tucker breathing on the other side. Crouching low, he slammed the door open and rolled inside the room. At first he couldn't see anything. The room was dark and the shadows hid most of the interior. After his initial movement, Sam froze. If Tucker was there, he didn't want to feel the sharp sting of his blade anywhere on his body.

Sam looked around from his position on the floor. He couldn't hear anything, and he was disappointed. He'd thought Tucker would be on this boat. He almost gave away his own position, and then something made him pause.

"Well, well, well, look who's come to play," Tucker whispered softly.

Sam followed the whisper and found himself looking into Tucker's dark eyes. His own eyes hardened into flint and he grabbed his gun a little tighter.

"So this is how it's going to end—you and me locked in mortal combat," Tucker said softly. "I often wondered about that."

"Only one of us will walk away from this," Sam assured him.

"Yes, I know," Tucker told him. "But you have the advantage—you have a gun, and all I have is a knife."

"You've always had things your own way before. You've always used the night shadows to escape before we knew what happened. Now the odds are against you," Sam said. Tucker stopped when Sam motioned him back.

Tucker raised an eyebrow at Sam. "Is that what you think? That the odds of my escape are out of my reach?"

"I know they are. Drop the knife or I'll drop you right here and now," Sam said quietly. He took a moment to cock his weapon. The sound echoed in the silence.

"You're going to have to shoot me to get this knife out of my hand," Tucker told him. He was counting on the fact that being a cop would make Sam want to take him in rather than shoot him. Sam was a cop first, an avenger second. "I guess it's been there too long to give it up now."

"As long as you have it in your hand, I can shoot you in self-defense," Sam reminded him.

Tucker laughed out loud. "As a police officer, you have to take me in and let the court decide my fate. You won't shoot me."

Sam's fingers tightened on his gun. It would be so easy to fire it and let the chips fall where they may. No one could blame him—after all, this was the man who'd kidnapped his son and murdered his wife. He would make sure the knife was still in Tucker's hand when the proper authorities found his body. Sam was sure he wouldn't lose any sleep over killing him. A man like Tucker Briggs deserved to die. But Sam had to know something first. "What did you mean back in the barn when you asked if I didn't know yet what you were planning?"

Tucker grinned. "I already told you. I wanted to know if you were clever enough to figure out the game we've been playing. I've been playing the game a long time now, and I wanted to see if there was anyone out there who could get close enough to stop me. I've had others try and join in on the game, but you were the best one so far. You got the closest of any of them. Maybe none of them cared as much as you did."

Sam frowned. "This was just your idea of a game?"

Tucker chuckled. "Sure. Only one problem, though— you don't like to play games, do you?"

Sam raised an eyebrow. "I don't like to play with people's lives, if that's what you're saying."

"But that's the fun part," Tucker told him as he wet his lips with his tongue. "I picked you for this particular game because you were the best cop I'd run into over the years. I got tired of the way the others left the game, so I just gave you a little extra incentive by taking your wife's life before the game started—that's all. I wanted to see if you could stop me, and you failed."

"Oh yeah, then why is my gun pointed right at you? I don't consider that a failure," Sam pointed out. "And you're right about the incentive part. You murdered my wife and took my son. After that there was no way I wasn't coming after you."

Tucker shook his head. "Yeah, but you have plans to take me in, and then things will get messy with a judge and a jury. I can't allow that to happen. I made up my mind to that a long time ago. I'd rather be dead than in jail, and you're too much of a cop to just shoot me. I'll walk away from this encounter, and after a while I'll go back to killing people again. You are just like all the others."

Tucker eased his way closer to the door. He was clearly confident in his assessment of Sam's character. He paused and looked at Sam. But Sam's resolve wasn't weakening.

Tucker played one last card. He grew impatient and snarled, "If you're going to shoot me, then shoot me. What are you waiting for?"

Sam hesitated and watched as Tucker's snarl turned into a sneer. "You're about as worthless as a screen door on a submarine, you and the rest of the world. No one has any guts anymore." Tucker turned and began walking toward the door.

"Tucker Briggs," Sam shouted, "turn around!"

Tucker turned to face Sam. The knife in his hands was raised to a defensive position. Sam could see that he was ready to charge at him, and Sam didn't hesitate. His index finger tightened slightly, and the gun in his hand exploded.

A surprised Tucker looked down at his chest. Blood

stained his shirt. He hadn't expected this turn of events. He had been so sure that Sam wouldn't shoot.

Tucker fell to his knees. His breathing was shallow, and as he tried to suck in more air, the blood gurgled in the back of his throat. He began choking on it, and as he coughed, blood spewed from his mouth. He fell to the floor and tried to speak, but the words wouldn't come. He couldn't catch his breath, and finally there was silence. Tucker Briggs was dead.

Sam moved away from the shadows and stood over Tucker's body. Tucker's eyes were open and blood dribbled from the corner of his mouth. The front of his shirt was red with blood. Sam reached for his neck but didn't find a pulse. He kicked the knife out of Tucker's hand and leaned down to check his pulse. There was none.

The boat rocked as Cole jumped aboard, and Sam met him at the door. Cole took one look at his face and backed away to let Sam up on deck. He disappeared below for a minute, then came back and joined Sam.

"Well, it's over this time for sure. Tucker won't hurt anyone else ever again," Cole said.

"I didn't have a choice. He had the knife in his hand, and he was coming for me. I didn't want to shoot him. I wanted to take him in. I hope you understand that," Sam told him. "He said that the game was really to find out if anyone could stop him. He told me that others have tried but that no one ever got as close as we did, and that no one ever kept coming like we did. He killed Chloe and took Wyatt to test me, to see how far I would go to get him back. He had such a look of stunned disbelief on his face when I shot him. He didn't think I would do it."

Cole looked at Sam and could read the truth in his eyes. "I know. There was something different about Tucker, and nobody knew what to do about it. He died the way he lived, on his own terms. Maybe this was the way it had to end the whole time. Maybe Tucker was right in his choice. He knew you wouldn't let him go. Maybe you were the only one who could stop him all along."

Sam looked at Cole and then at the doorway that led belowdecks. "We'd better call John Sanders. He'll want to be notified that there is a body now."

Sam left the boat and walked to the water's edge. His nightmare was finally over. He had a lot to make up for, but killing Tucker had been necessary. Suddenly, Sam couldn't wait to see his son. He wanted to feel Wyatt's arms around his neck again. Life without Chloe would be hard, but at least he still had Wyatt, and he knew they would somehow make it. They had both lost so much in the last few weeks, but together they would survive.